SAINTS,
UNEXPECTED

SAINTS, UNEXPECTED

Brent van Staalduinen

For Colleen's dearest brother in law God. All my best wishes.

10.26.2016

Novel Ideas!

Invisible Publishing
Halifax & Toronto

Library and Archives Canada Cataloguing in Publication

Van Staalduinen, Brent, 1973-, author
    Saints unexpected / Brent van Staalduinen.

Issued in print and electronic formats.
ISBN 978-1-926743-72-1 (paperback).--ISBN 978-1-926743-73-8 (epub).--
ISBN 978-1-926743-74-5 (mobi)

    I. Title.

PS8643.A598S23 2016   C813'.6   C2016-900943-2
                                               C2016-900944-0

Edited by Leigh Nash
Cover & Interior designed by Megan Fildes

Typeset in Laurentian and Gibson by Megan Fildes
With thanks to type designer Rod McDonald

Printed and bound in Canada

Invisible Publishing | Halifax & Toronto
www.invisiblepublishing.com

We acknowledge the support of the Canada Council for the Arts, which last year
invested $157 million to bring the arts to Canadians throughout the country.

Canada Council   Conseil des Arts
for the Arts   du Canada

For Rosalee.
My Left,
my love.

The city shakes so subtly, we sometimes mistake it
for the ghost of its ambition, the effect of our work
the force of our breath in the night.

— Chris Pannell, "A Nervous City"

————————————————

Love is so short, forgetting is so long.

— Pablo Neruda

HAMILTON, THEN

We left the front door open. We never left it open.

Leich and I opened Second Chances, my mother's thrift store, like we usually did, with a quick sweep and dust, and the counting of the day's float. It was a Monday, so the cash register held only fifty dollars. There was little reason to keep more on hand. If you did business in downtown Hamilton, you learned about slow Monday mornings. Our store opened at eight to catch a few of the business folk before work, but the shelters and halfway houses, which supplied much of the foot traffic in our neighbourhood, didn't start kicking people out until after eleven. My mother, Anne, said she set up the hours that way to catch the first wave of white collars, the keen ones who get downtown early for the free parking spots on the east side. But it was a bit of a dream, really, trying to entice bleary worker drones as they trudged towards huddled office buildings with what she called "pre-chanced" things.

There was a heavy clunk from the storeroom as Leich—think "like" when you say it—opened the safe. The door always thunked against the drywall partition between the storefront and the back room. We told Mom that we should move the safe to save the wall, but she never did. So the drywall crumbled, like drywall always seems to do.

— Hey, Mutts, did you get to the bank on Friday?

— No, I said.

— We're almost out of loonies.

— Mom said we'd be fine.

— She's not the one running out of change in the middle of the day.

— We're not in the middle of the jungle.

— Says you.

I rolled my eyes, took the window cleaner and a cloth from behind the till, and walked to the front door. Through the fingerprints and smudges, the morning traffic on King Street had begun to build. I opened the door and sprayed the outside glass, dissolving the weekend grime. How dirty the main display windows were; we had hired someone to clean them on Sunday nights, but it looked as though he had decided to take the weekend off. I knew Mom would be pissed about that. Leich came to the front and rattled the cash drawer into the old register, slamming it twice before it caught. He turned the register key and the machine whirred and clicked to life.

— It's a good one today, he said, stepping out onto the sidewalk beside me.

— Yeah, you can't even smell the mills.

— No, dummy, I meant this.

He handed over the Niche's offering for the day, a hinged silver box the size of a deck of cards. Although it was tarnished, it was heavy and lined with purple silk, which gave it a regal air, and was covered in ornate designs.

— Nice, I said. Especially the—

Although I knew that the silver and silk were real—the Niche's offerings always were—the proper term for the designs escaped me. Reliefs? Embossings? Carvings? Engravings? I frowned, annoyed at myself, the writer, for questioning the word.

Leich didn't notice. He stretched and breathed.

— You weren't kidding, he said. It smells great.

— Can't remember the last time the sky was so blue, either.

— Such a romantic. You must have to fight them off.

I punched him on the arm.

Our city was still a steel town in those days. The two mills, north and east of the downtown, ran three shifts, and we knew when the wind changed. The fumes spewed from the smelters and burn offs were the worst in the summer, when the heat and humidity kept the smog low to the ground, wreathing the downtown in the smell of overheated brake pads. The city had mourned the loss of jobs when one of the mills closed down a few years earlier, then rejoiced when it opened again under different ownership. A foreign corporation promised change and profits and renewal. The endless cycle of boom and bust. Regardless, nothing helped with the smell. Probably the pollution, too, but there was an almost mythical belief in the city that Hamiltonians had stronger lungs than anyone.

I suggested we leave the door open to air things out a bit. As the slightest breath of westerly wind blew down the sidewalk, fresh and clear, Leich hesitated for an instant, then nodded.

You didn't leave your door open on King Street. We had all sorts of community action groups trumpeting the successes of their efforts towards urban renewal, with progress and money creeping east, but our stretch of King hadn't changed much. Then—I don't know about now, as I haven't been back for more than twenty years—much of the visible population was every shade of poor, from the destitute to the barely scraping by. There were a number of shelters, soup kitchens, and missions in our neighbourhood, so addicts and homeless people wandered around everyone else in a parade of need. We closed our doors against them hoping, along with every other small business, that the real buyers knew enough—were confident enough—to come inside.

Still, we could deal with the wandering and homeless. All it took was a request to leave and they would, or a nudge on the shoulder to rouse them from their stupor. Rarely, we might have had to call the police, or the hotlines for one of the city services if a drunk had a rehab card pinned to his coat. *If found, and I can't answer, call the Shepherds of Immaculate Hope at 906-767-8724. Thank you kindly!* I had lots of stories like that. In fact, the best stories in my journal came from dealing with our city's most needy people, stories I hoped to make use of someday. When I got back to writing, that was.

Leich grabbed the box and began buffing it with the hem of his T-shirt.

— I'll put it somewhere, he said.

— I know where it's going.

— You do, eh?

— You have no imagination. Predictable.

— Uh-huh. Speaking of which, is today the day you crack your diary open for the first time in forever?

— I told you, it's not a diary —

— True. Diaries get written in, don't they?

— I'm just waiting for the right words.

I wasn't sure if that was true or not. I wasn't sure what I was waiting for—though there was a short story in the back of my mind that I'd been wanting to write for weeks, no matter how many times I'd opened the black, hardcover notebook nothing came out.

— Well, don't wait too long, he said, holding up the silver
  box and heading back inside.

This was the game, our summer ritual for the few weeks
we ran the store. We took turns finding a place for whatever the Niche gave us, and tried to predict when it would
be found, by whom, and what his or her story would be.
The Niche was our family name for the cubbyhole at the
back of the store. We theorized that the Niche, with its
bricked-up rear wall and insulated, in-swinging door, had
originally opened into the alley, a leftover from the days
of milk delivery. Every morning, it delivered a single item
meant for one person, the kind of thing everyone hopes
to find when they browse a thrift store: the perfect trinket,
keepsake, or heirloom-to-be. You might wander into a
place like Second Chances looking for a pair of pants, a
belt, or a practical, needed item, but you're also hoping to
find something more. Also a given is that what you want
to find is rarely what you need, and the Niche seemed
to know this—its item was always discovered and the
customer always left happy. Without fail, the item was
destined for the person who needed it most.

There had never been a day when the store was open
that the Niche item had gone unsold. So as usual I went
behind the register and closed my eyes, trying to come
up with my story before Leich came back to the front.
Nothing. Not even a glimmer of inspiration. I told myself
that it must be because I was distracted by the possibilities
ahead of me. School had just let out for the summer, all I
faced was three months of writing and helping at the store,
and it was a clear, lovely day outside. I might have called
those possibilities romantic, but in a chaste, old-school
way, where reading a good book surrounded by fields of

flowers is enough to hold a fifteen-year-old's desires. Or, in my case, taking in good literature on our apartment stoop, with the sidewalks my pastures and the buildings my trees. Do teenage girls—does anyone, really—ever think about those things any more?

— Gimme the money or you're fucking dead!

I opened my eyes to the business end of a gun. People say that time slows down when they're in danger, or that their life flashes before their eyes, but that wasn't true for me. The muzzle of the gun was huge and black and his finger on the trigger was very much in real time. I screamed.

— Shut up! The money, now!

The freezing you hear about, though, was real. I couldn't even twitch. I stopped, fear cutting off my scream like a blade, and I was afraid that my inability to move would be what killed me. That's when I noticed the man's hair, so incredibly blond, like a beacon shining from beyond the gun's black muzzle.

— Hey, take it easy, boss, Leich said, amazingly calm, somewhere off to my side.

The robber swung the gun towards my brother, who was standing with his hands up between the coat rack and the CD shelf. Although my voice box was mute, inside I was still screaming, thinking about the gun pointed at my big brother's face.

— Don't move! The money!

— You can have it all, but can I go to the register? My sister's too scared to move.

— Okay, but if you do anything stupid, I'll kill her, the guy said, jabbing the gun at me for emphasis.

I wet myself.

— All right, man, no probl—

Leich's voice, so stable until that instant, cracked when he saw the dark spot spreading down the front of my jeans. He moved to the cash register. There was a horrible moment when he hit the No Sale button and the catch wouldn't release, but on his second try the drawer chattered open. He stepped back, putting his arm around my shoulders. It was warm. He'd tell me later I was trembling enough to shake both of us.

The man reached over the counter and helped himself. He thumbed through the meagre pile of bills and groaned before stuffing them into his pocket. His eyes darted around the room as his mind tallied up the paltry sum. For a long time I assumed that what he thought in that moment was that the money wasn't enough to justify the risk, worrying perhaps about being arrested. But the later, clearer memories of his dark, yellow-tinged skin, the circles under his eyes, and the stretched sinews in his neck, made it clear that jail wasn't on his mind. Robbing a second-hand store with a gun at eight on a Monday morning had nothing to do with the money at all, really, but a deeper, more chemical need.

— What about the back? You got a safe?

— Yeah, Leich said. I'll take you.

But there's nothing else there, I thought.

— Okay, but don't try anything.

The man gestured towards the back, the sudden movement making something in the gun rattle. Bullets, maybe. Or the cylinder. Why was I so focused on the noise? Leich led him back to the storeroom and they disappeared. I imagined my brother kneeling in front of the safe and entering the six-digit code and the door swinging open to an empty safe. Clunk. The door against the drywall. A couple of ledgers and an empty money shelf. I wonder if the darkness of the empty safe made as much of an impact on the desperate man as the muzzle of the gun had on me. I wonder what he saw, whether it was an end, or a beginning, or nothing at all.

He yelled a frustrated obscenity that echoed through the store. A second. A third. He pushed my brother back towards the front and screamed curses at whatever future he was seeing. Leich's eyes, wide and red, met mine. The man stomped forward, running his pistol across a shelf, clearing it of curios and knick-knacks in one violent, frustrated swath.

— I can't believe this shit, he said. I should have known— why am I here?

His voice was strained but he looked distant, like an actor speaking with someone just off-screen, his eyes moving from the door to the walls to the mess on the floor to the two of us behind the counter. He made a decision.

— Your phones, wallets, jewelry. Now!

Leich put his new phone on the counter, followed by his wallet. I still couldn't move. The robber snatched Leich's things and stuffed them into the front pocket of his filthy sweatshirt. He looked at me. Nothing. My hands were like lead. He jabbed the gun towards me again. Leich moved, reaching in front of me, and I wondered if he was still trying to protect me or grab my things. His movement must have threatened the man, because he lunged over the counter and clipped Leich on his temple with the gun. Leich fell against the wall, stunned, a bead of blood running down the side of his face, bright red, fast.

Did I move then? No. Not even a little.

The man saw he had crossed a line. A feverish glance at my brother. A half turn towards the open door. A half turn back. He raised his gun again, and a strange certainty moved across his features, angry and dark. Right there, right then.

That was the moment. The moment that stretched between us and the guy who had ripped our morning apart. You can't go back, can't unmake wrongs, can't erase anything. But you try. He raised the gun. He would now try.

We're going to die, I thought.

Leich moaned. The robber looked at him and his eyes changed, like he'd finally seen Leich's blood. He shook his head like he was trying to clear it, howled a final curse, and clenched his fists. The gun went off, the clang of a dropped pot, only a thousand times bigger. Time shifted then. A tiny blink of bluish flame popped from the muzzle. A puff of dust and a quarter-sized hole appeared in the drywall at the back. The deafening report. The recoil knocked the gun from his hand. All of us stood, shaking, listening to the sound of everything changing. An instant, all of it, but one that would stretch out across every second for the rest of the summer.

He fell to his knees and scrabbled through the things he had swept onto the floor. His hand found the gun but, just as he was about to stand, something must have caught his eye because he stopped and his hand reached straight for the little silver box from the Niche. He stood a moment, dazed by the gorgeous decorations, before jerkily stuffing it into the pocket of his cargos. He jabbed the gun at each of us a final time, punctuating the echoes with an unspoken, monumental threat, then fled into the bright morning sunlight.

A bluish haze lingered, the air inside the store smelling like hot steel, unpurified by the open door and clean breeze outside. I collapsed against the wall beside Leich, knocking to the floor the old sepia photograph of our building, a gift from the local BIA, which had hung behind the cash register since the store's opening. It landed on its corner, cracks bursting outwards in a fractured sunrise.

Later, we'd ask each other if we were all right. Right then, though, as the adrenaline wore off, we just sat next to each other, shaking and nauseated, not speaking. I began to cry, but I couldn't bring myself to look at my bleeding, heroic brother to see if he was crying too.

Mom was so fixated on the store having to close that she didn't even notice the cop—a short man who seemed to enjoy the puffed-up look his bulletproof vest gave him, like he had a chest under there somewhere—flirting with her. Someone had heard the gunshot and called 911, and the police arrived within a minute or two. Back then, you didn't have to go far to find a cop downtown—they hovered, especially east of James. Another five minutes saw four cruisers, an ambulance, and a large, black tactical truck parked out front on King Street, splashing Second Chances and the other shops in our row with cherry flashing lights.

— Closed for how long?
— Ma'am, let's just take this one step at a time. There has been a shooting, after all.
— For. How. Long?

The cop missed my mother's tone and held up his hands with a smile.

— Not my call, I'm afraid. But I'm sure they'll come running back to see you, ma'am.

Yes, he was that obvious.

My ears felt like they'd been blocked by cotton, making every conversation sound like it was happening through a door. It was frustrating how everyone else used their normal voices, leaving me to yell at them to speak up. The buzz of activity around the store was disorienting, too; my mind had begun to push more and more pieces of the crime into my subconscious, detaching me, memory by memory, from what had just happened. My mother arrived about thirty minutes after the robbery. Leich had called her with my phone after we'd collected ourselves, interrupting one of Wu's weekly appointments at St. Joseph's Hospital. She came as quickly as she could, arriving to find the store swarming with emergency personnel and her two oldest children wrapped in blankets and sitting on the grimy curb. She asked if we were all right, left Wu—my three-year-old brother—with us, and walked inside without waiting for an answer.

For Wu, it was Christmas: uniformed people running around, the flashing lights, the vehicles. He sat in his stroller mesmerized by the activity, swivelling his bald, wrinkled head around, his eyes wide with excitement, peppering us with questions. Because my hearing was so bad, Leich had taken over responding to Wu's questions—I had practically startled the poor little guy out of his Pull-Ups by yelling *What?* at him after his first. Aside from my broken hearing, I was still unsteady and queasy from the robbery, and surviving one breath at a time was about all I could manage. It was great that Leich still had it in him to make sure my sick baby brother was fed a steady diet of big brother patience.

Wu had progeria, an extremely rare disease that accelerated his age right from birth, making him look like an old man in kid's clothing. He had all the symptoms: hardening tissue, premature aging of skin, arteriosclerosis. And strokes. Wu had already had two of them, which accounted for his weekly checkups at St. Joe's, the dark circles under my mother's eyes, and perhaps her absent-mindedness towards Leich and me at the crime scene.

— Look at the lights, Wu. Have you ever seen lights like that?

— Police truck!

— Police *car*, buddy. Firemen ride trucks.

— Fireman car!

Leich made a face. Wu giggled, quite satisfied.

I wanted to smile too, be easy, but it was tiring to decipher the muddy conversations all around me. So I watched the activity instead. The motorists on King Street, which had been reduced to one lane because of our robbery investigation, were throwing dirty looks our way. Commuters usually blasted along King, a one-way thoroughfare with synchronized stoplights, like it was a freeway, so the backup was extensive. The pedestrians too had been stopped by police and were being forced to pass through Gore Park on the opposite side of King. They looked put out.

I didn't much care about the angry motorists—so few of them stopped as they burned through downtown—but the pedestrians were mostly folks from our neighbourhood, our customers, our friends. They should have been used to closed sidewalks and detours, the daily adjustments of urban life. I was also annoyed at Mom's indifference towards us after the robbery, yet still hoped the neighbourhood wouldn't take it out on her and Second Chances. She was already exhausted so much of the time, with a sick kid needing almost full-time care and running a business. A business that struggled, given the location and the economic realities of our neighbourhood, to stay in the black month after month.

She walked out of the store, trailed by the police officer with his too-big vest and notebook. When Wu saw her, he did what he always did when he saw one of us. He scrunched up his face, balled his wrinkled hands and brought them close to his chest, screwed his goggle eyes tight, and tensed for a split second before bursting his body open and raising his hands over his shoulders. He smiled then, so big and bright you'd swear the wrinkles disappeared.

— Yay! Mommy!

He always said Yay! as loudly as he could. It was the cutest thing in the history of cute things, and never failed to bring a smile to our faces—all of us, even my mother, who carried so much worry. To this day, I well up when I think of it, how pure and joyful Wu was, and how easily we lose that joy when we get older.

Mom smiled briefly at Wu before turning back to the officer, who was talking to her back. She stopped smiling.

— I beg your pardon?

The officer, clueless, grinned and pointed at Leich and me. He said something I didn't catch, although his mouth looked like it was forming the words, great kids! I shrugged. He faced me, put his hands around his mouth and yelled, like I was clear across town rather than a few feet away. His voice was loud, even through my stopped-up ears.

— IT WAS A SMALL GUN, AS FAR AS GUNS GO!

Two other cops standing nearby—a male and a female— nodded their agreement. They looked big to me, although it was probably their uniforms. Hamilton cops wore black uniforms that made the big ones look huge and everyone else like they were trying too hard. The small cop, smiling again for his comrades, didn't need the vest or the dark clothes, though—when you tell a girl on the sunny side of fifteen that the gun that went off three feet from her face is a small one, you're trying too hard.

My mother said something too soft for me to hear. The cop's face fell. He closed his book, turned slowly, and walked back into the store without another word. Leich picked Wu up, Mom folded the stroller, and the four of us walked to the barred door next to Second Chances. I dug out my key, threw the deadbolt, and held open the door to the stairway that led to our apartment above the store. Before following Leich and Wu into the gloom, my mother paused for an instant, ran her eyes from my hair to my stomach to my shoes and shook her head, her face expressionless. I watched her legs and back as she ascended to the apartment, wondering why she'd stopped and what message she expected me to decipher. I had no idea. I just closed the heavy door behind us, the red flashing lights narrowing to a thin strip of dancing light and then nothing at all.

I woke up on the couch with an earache, but able to hear again. The sun hadn't yet risen so the living room was quiet and dark. Someone had turned the lights off while I slept. I got up, tied my hair back, and padded into the kitchen. In the dim light cast by the range hood, as the fridge hummed its quiet, insistent tune, I spooned back some cereal, holding the bowl above the sink to protect the hardwood floor from soggy drippings. I didn't look any different, I thought, staring at a ghostly, suspended reflection of myself against the dark city outside. But should I? An occasional set of headlights zipped through my dark reflection, racing down King like impatient, earthbound stars.

I had tuned everyone out for the rest of the previous day and evening, first exhausted by the constant effort of listening to what they were saying and later depressed by the hard, argumentative tones that bled through the ringing in my ears. My father had arrived home at his usual time, which always fell between dinner and bedtime. He couldn't believe no one had called him about the robbery and argued with my mother about it.

I think she waited for certain moments to get mad at him just to have some release. Betrayal can linger. Dad vanished in the summer of 2005 without a note or even a phone call, leaving the three of us hurting and wondering who he had run from. He came back after three years, remorseful as Judas, and my mother forgave him in front of Leich and me, for our benefit, I'm sure. But despite his indiscretion—much later, I would learn more about his affair, which only lasted a few months, the rest of the time spent alone in purgatory, searching for the courage to face us—my father was a good man, and in time her show of forgiveness became genuine. Wu was born healthy and bright a year after Dad returned—the nicest kind of surprise to come out of such a bitter time—but was diagnosed at eighteen months old, changing every routine we had. Second Chances had never made much money, but the constant appointments and hospital visits had made Mom's armour brittle, cracking in tense moments like on the day of the robbery.

They had argued last night, even though my dad, as much as he had to atone for, was perfectly in the right to be upset that no one had called him right away about the robbery. I was still mad at her, but between my fractured emotional state and hearing loss, I was too unsettled to take sides, right or wrong. When they carried their argument to their bedroom, I fell asleep on the sofa.

— You didn't say much last night, my mother said as she came into the kitchen, surprising me.

— Listening is too much work sometimes. Even I could hear that you and Dad got into it pretty deep.

— Do you remember anything?

— Bits and pieces. I know they're part of the robbery, but they don't seem connected to anything right now.

— I'm sure it'll come back.

Do I really want it to? I wanted to ask.

— Yeah, I said instead.

— Your hearing seems better. How do your ears feel?

She moved past me, turned on the under-cabinet lighting, and started pulling her tea things from the cupboard. My mother looked young for her age, attractive and lithe even after three kids and a few years of bearing the worries of a small business. She had unruly auburn hair that always looked like it was trying to escape from whatever she tied it back with, as though blaming her for its own worries. Perfect hippie hair, an accessory to the jeans and loose shirts she wore, and drew attention from her extra-fair skin and the dark shadows under her eyes. Dad had dark hair, almost black, dark enough to slick back and get away with, although he preferred styles that made him invisible everywhere except the courtroom. When they took rare moments together in the kitchen or in the store's back room, their heads were fire and crude oil, enough to make a person wonder how he had tamed her fiery mane. I have mousy light brown hair and still wonder where the heck it came from.

Her reflection stopped and looked at me. Waited for a response. Surprise, surprise, Mutton, I thought. She did pay attention after all.

But I didn't speak right away, forcing her to hold out her olive branch until even its spindly weight felt heavy. The robbery felt too fresh, how she'd barely paused to make sure if Leich and I were all right, jumping right into concern for the store, revenues lost, inventory damaged. Instead, I studied a street cleaner working the east corner of the park. Enough light made it across, even in the pre-dawn darkness, that the reflective strips on his chartreuse safety suit danced, suspended, like those bizarre fish who live so deep in the ocean they have to make their own light. That was me, making my own light, wondering if anyone watched for it. I couldn't see the cleaner's face, though. That was more like my family—a summer spent searching for each other, our night vision ruined by harsh, unexpected reflections.

— Sure, I can hear fine, I said.

— Oh, that's good. I was worried—

— But they really hurt.

I said it with weight. *Hurt.* There was a brief bloom of satisfaction until I heard Mom's sharp intake of breath behind me and the heavy clunking of ceramic on the countertop. Shifting my vision slightly, I saw her shoulders tremble as she placed both hands on the counter beside the can of loose tea and the mug, as though she needed help to stay upright. She was crying, but I didn't turn from the window, even as she continued to sob, soundless, in the dim kitchen light. There are few things harder to hear than a loved one caught between needing to cry and not making a sound. The sound is so important; you can't release yourself fully without it. Now I wanted to reach out and comfort her, but I didn't. On one hand, I wanted her to be crying right then—I wanted her to feel bad—but on the other, even my teenage self knew how hard things had been for her. Neither of us spoke.

Heavy steps clumped into the kitchen, accompanied by exaggerated sounds of yawning and stretching. Leich made straight for the fridge, opened it, and stared into it for a long moment, clueless, as my mother wiped her eyes and filled the kettle. The white bandage on his temple covering his three stitches—a fresh, blood-free dressing, I was grateful to see—was bright in the fridge's half-hearted light. He grunted, scratched himself, and slammed the door before grabbing the box of cereal I'd left out and digging in for a handful.

— You're both up early, he said. Couldn't sleep?

— No, Mom said, finding her voice. Wu was up twice—
  all the excitement, I suppose.

— I crashed hard and slept like a baby, Leich said.

— That's surprising.

— I thought so, too. But then, a few minutes ago, every thing inside me just blinked on. I was as wide awake as if I'd never slept. Funny, eh?

— At least I won't have to drag you out of bed, she said.

There was a pause in the conversation. I took my bowl over to the sink, feeling their eyes on my back as they waited for my participation. One last bit of cereal, soggy and disintegrating, clung doggedly to the bowl's inside. I spent too much time pulverizing it with the dish brush. Easier than speaking, though.

— I'll open the store today, Mutts, Leich said. So you can go back to your beauty sleep.

He delivered the lines like they were a gift from a magnanimous king, dropping Mutts in to bug me. It worked, of course. I hated when he called me that, telling myself that my writing career in Toronto would be jeopardized by a nickname, even though my real name was challenge enough. I turned and flung some dishwater at him with the brush, making him laugh. My mother smiled, too, although the low light accentuated the shadows on her face, making her look even more thin and tired.

— I wonder if the police will be finished, she said.

— Such a big deal for just another robbery, Leich said, rolling his eyes.

It might have been genuine, his bravado. He had seemed so calm while the robber was in the store, but I had felt him shaking before the police arrived. Seventeen years and the bright potential of the future didn't take away the fact that he was still just a teenager, albeit one who seemed to grow more certain of his steps while I just stumbled along. He had gotten taller over the previous few months, which suited him well, unlike the gangly results of his first pubescent growth spurt a few years before. I could see that my brother, although never particularly athletic, was growing into what he would become. When they talk about boys filling out, you don't often think about the insides filling out as well, about the confidence and attitude that turns boys into men. Leich was, though; even his mop of hair, mousy like mine, seemed somehow to frame his face in a new way, like it fit. My mother, although trying to do better to respect his growing independence, still saw him as a boy. Her boy.

— Not with gunfire, it wasn't, she said.

— It was an accident.

— Leich, he carried the gun into my store and shot through my wall. That's no accident.

— *Your* wall? *Your* store?

— Yes, Mutton, my wall, my store. What's with you?

— Nothing, I said. It's just that—

And I ran out of words, caught in that strange gap between anger and the inability to express it. Leich filled it for me, reading me like a big brother.

— We were there, Mom, he said quietly.

Mom fell silent and dropped a bag of green tea into her mug. She lifted the kettle, poured the scalding water, and stirred. A long moment passed, punctuated only by the sound of her spoon moving in circles, Leich's hand plunging into the cereal box, and the crunching of dry cereal in his mouth. He looked at the floor, chewing hard, his eyes far away, betraying him. Standing up for me had brought back the robbery closer than he'd anticipated, knocking his bravado aside.

— Maybe we should leave the store closed for the day, I said.

No one said anything to that for another long moment, until my mother shook her head, moving beside me to dump her still-hot, untasted tea into the sink.

— No, she said. You two can take care of Wu and I'll open up.

— Did you finish at St. Joe's yesterday?

Leich's question made her stop mid-pour and whisper a quiet expletive. It wasn't a question of divided loyalties— there was no doubt about my mother's commitment to our baby brother—but just a brief, crass acknowledgment of how her simple life had changed. A store in trouble. A fractured marriage. A wonderful yet sickly addition to our family. Her part in the family paradox, a cord braided together by good and bad, each member a distinct strand but stronger together, misunderstood yet understood by no one better. And there were never enough minutes or seconds in a day to deal with the challenges.

She swore again and said that we would have to open as planned, provided the police okayed it. Leich closed the cereal box and put it on the counter behind him.

— I've been thinking about deferring my acceptance to help out with the store, he said.

His proclamation came out of nowhere. I bet my mother and I mirrored each other's expression: shock with a tinge of horror. He had been accepted to study pre-law at UBC, one of the best programs in the country, on a full scholarship, a huge honour. Dad had been over the moon about it, even though his law school alma mater was U of T and he would have loved for Leich to tread the same path. Leich had made a show of singing the program's praises as the reason he had looked so far west, but we all knew that the distance had been the real draw. When you have a couple of retired hippies for parents who've travelled all over for protest this and cause that, it's hard not to be infected by their lives of adventure. They had such great stories, ones they used to tell all the time before Dad left. After, well, not so much. Seeds had been planted, though, and I had answered the call by creating different worlds in my journal while my older brother looked at travel websites and law school to pay for it all.

Leich read our faces and held up his hands.

— Just for a while, until Wu is off to school and you can get back to normal, he said.

— Absolutely not. I'd shut down the store before I'd let that happen.

— Mom, they'll hold my scholarship—

— Leich, no. End of discussion.

Hippies never tell others that the discussion is ended. Mom using those words, so final, so unlike the openness they tried to foster in our home, landed like a gavel in court. Leich wasn't trying to be difficult, he was just being the son they had raised, fighting in his own way for something he believed in. He wanted to make sure we were taken care of, but Mom didn't seem to get that. At least for a moment, because Leich recovered quickly, mad as anything, and he laid into her about being unfair, killing his freedom, and so on. Her summary dismissal—could she not even pretend to give it some thought?—fuelled my own anger, which twisted around my concern for her in tense, fishing-line knots.

Dad was in the kitchen in an instant, intent on keeping the peace, his housecoat flapping around him. Down the hall, we heard Wu wake up and start crying, a sound we didn't hear all that often any more, as though his emotions had matured early, too, deciding that his difficult, under-sized life was better filled with smiles. As I left, hoping to retreat into my room and close the door, Dad turned all the lights in the kitchen on, filling the windows with reflections of a family in conflict rather than the rising light of sunrise.

Peter, my best friend, was waiting for Leich and me when we went down to open the store, concern pasted across his face. He'd heard about the robbery but I hadn't invited him over, limiting our interaction to a couple of text messages establishing that I was fine, that no one had been hurt. There was an awkward moment where, as I was trying to dig the store keys out of my pocket, he tried to hug me, all shoulders and bones and apologies.

Leich asked Peter if he'd brought a phone.

— Oh, right, Peter said, handing over a shiny box.

— It looks brand new, I said.

— Four or five months old. My uncle, he—

— We know, Leich said. Newest of everything. You suffer through the handoffs. Blah, blah, blah.

I glared at my brother.

— Okay, okay, he said. Thanks, Peter.

Peter hadn't even noticed the slight. He beamed, perfectly pleased to help out.

The three of us stepped over to the store, where a long piece of yellow crime-scene tape trailed along the sidewalk, lifting and twisting in the slight wind. The front door had been propped open. A police van was parked along the street, and a bicycle cop in a neon yellow jacket was standing guard, leaning against the front window.

— He's with us, Leich said to the officer, nodding at Peter. Our, uh, employee.

The cop waved us in, barely looking up as Leich delivered his tiny white lie. On some of the mornings I opened the store, Peter would drop by to help us get ready for the day. He didn't work—his aunt and uncle, his guardians since his parents had been killed years before, gave him an allowance from his part of the insurance payout—so he enjoyed the break in his summer routine, which was mostly filled with texting me and building scale models of local buildings.

The store was filled with light from portable stands the forensics team had set up. Too bright. Every stain, dust bunny, and scuff on full display. A pair of technicians dressed in white hooded jumpsuits were packing gear into large plastic containers. A third was leaning against the cash register counter, tapping away on a laptop.

— How much more time do you think you'll need? Leich asked.

The guy didn't respond for a long moment.

— As much as it takes, he finally said.

— Will we be able to open on time?

— If we finish, sure.

One of the techs stood from the containers and walked over, gave the laptop guy a withering look, pulled back his hood, and stuck out a hand. He introduced himself as lead for the team and apologized for his colleague.

— He's just tired, he said. We'd hoped to be done by now. But it won't be much longer.

— Can we do anything? I asked.

— We're done out here, so you can get ready—we'll need a little more time in the back, though.

A little more time turned out to be a couple of hours. Leich, Peter, and I were able to clean up the mess quickly, but what took the most time was wiping down the ultra-fine black powder the forensics guys had dusted anywhere the robber might have touched. Finally, the technicians emerged, the two subordinates carrying the heavy cases and the lead guy holding the computer, as well as a sheaf of clear bags outlined in red and emblazoned across the front with EVIDENCE blocked out in black. I pointed at the outermost bag, which had a hunk of metal inside that looked like a tiny copper mushroom.

— Is that the bullet?

— Yep. Bugger to get out of the brick, too.

— It's so small, Peter said.

— A .38, I'd guess, but we won't know until we get it back to the lab.

His tone suggested we should know what he was talking about. While he explained that there was no more evidence to collect but that we needed to leave the bullet holes alone for the time being, his colleagues carried out the floodlights. After the blinding completeness of the portable lights, the store's regular fluorescents felt dim and dingy enough to make my eyes hurt. I followed the guy outside to give my vision a break. There was a change in atmosphere as I walked onto the sidewalk, the passing vehicles pushing the air hard against me, and my ears protested the pressure. As I tried opening and closing my mouth and swallowing to even things out, the bike cop came over, the crime-scene tape an unruly wad in his gloved hands, and said we were now allowed to open the store.

— He won't come back, he said. They almost never do.

Having made his proclamation—which was, no doubt, intended to reassure—he donned his helmet and rode away. He rang his handlebar bell for a couple of kids whose young, tired mother had brought them over to watch the crime-scene cleanup.

When I went back in, Peter and Leich were talking about that morning's Niche item, a small cup that looked like a miniature version of a chalice you might find on a medieval banquet table. Peter knew about the Niche, although I can't remember exactly when he figured it out. From time to time, like that morning, he'd come around while we were getting Second Chances ready and watch us play our game, on some days even accompanying me to the back to retrieve the item. Leich put it on a counter opposite the cash register so he could keep an eye on it.

— I had to remind him to get it, Peter said.

— I would've remembered.

Peter laughed.

— Is this the face of a guy who remembers?

Peter handed me his phone, the screen lit up with a photo. Leich had been caught in the back room with one hand reaching for the item and the other towards the camera, middle finger extended.

— Perfect, I said.

— I'll text you a copy, Peter said.

Leich tried to grab the phone. He hated that he'd been caught in a moment of weakness—I'd certainly never seen him flip anyone off—and even more so that he'd left evidence. Peter danced away from him and tapped on his screen. A few seconds later, there was a low, electronic buzzing against my backside and the chime of a text arriving. Leich shook his head.

— Just delete it, will you?

— Not a chance.

— Please?

Any other morning, I'd have savoured his begging. But there was a hollowness to his voice, like exhaustion but deeper, a dangerous resignation. Peter sensed it, too, and just before leaving offered to erase the original from his phone.

Leich and I had a quiet morning in the store. We had a few customers stop in, but everyone seemed more interested in talking about the robbery than buying anything. Mom took over at noon, leaving Wu with me for the rest of the day. She wasn't happy that we'd opened late, and even less pleased that we had to leave the bullet damage alone. She ranted about how customers notice details like that, how it doesn't take much to drive people away. Gunfire was pretty good at doing that on its own, I thought but didn't say. Bullets, too— they punched through walls and embedded themselves in brick, got dug out and sealed away in evidence bags. Their weight, too, mushroomed and heavy, carried around in a girl's gut if she thought about them too much.

That night, I walked slowly through the lengthening shadows in the park to Duster's, the pub where the Guild, my writer's group, gathered. Guild meetings were held on the first Tuesday of every month—that night's meeting had been circled in red on my mental calendar, as I'd been looking forward to receiving advice about my incubating short story. The lingering trauma of the robbery and that morning's family tension had knocked some of the wind out of me, though, and I almost hadn't gone. The silence of our apartment drove me out. Mom and Dad had tried to ask us about the rest of our day, maintaining our usual dinnertime rhythm, but Leich refused to supply more than grunts and single words. I hadn't been in the mood to make small talk. Even Wu was quiet. I needed to spend some time away from my family, even if it meant sitting through a Guild meeting without having anything to contribute.

Duster's was a popular place, its highlight being a long wooden bar lined by beer taps from all over the world. A bell above the door tinkled when I came in, drawing glances from the seated regulars. A couple of older men dressed in black suits held court at the bar, their features nearly identical apart from a spread of years. Father and son. They looked sad. Jenny—Duster's manager, a stout, foul woman who always seemed to be squinting—gave me a quick nod as she placed a couple of fresh pints in front of the men, which they tipped towards each other before taking long, deep draughts.

The Guild was like my other family, a family that better understood my need to retreat into the pages of a journal or the characters in a book. A few years before, I had seen a flyer in the window of Duster's and got over my nerves just enough to call the listed number. Eleanor, the organizer, told me to walk right to the back of the bar where I would see everyone with their laptops and notebooks and piles of scattered paper. My feet took me inside, but no further, as though they had second thoughts about carrying an eleven-year-old into a bar. Thankfully, Eleanor saw me trembling beside the bar and rescued me. I spent the entire first meeting quiet and nervous, wondering when the group would throw Junior out to spare the adults from her inexperience. That never happened. They even asked my opinion a few times. Imagine that.

My excitement had been so great for the next month's meeting that I brought the true story of my family carefully written in a mint green Hilroy notebook. How my parents met at an anti-Gulf War rally in 1990 to the day in '05 when Dad left, and much in between. Dad returned, his tail between his legs, a few months later, but his betrayal still burned so much that I only used his first name. *Michael*

left us, I wrote. The Guild noticed this little bit of objecti-
fication, praising its literary impact and commenting on
the maturity of my prose. Cementing, in that same breath,
my devotion to the group. We all crave inclusion, don't
we, especially as we stumble through our teenage years?
One Thursday night, away from siblings, the store, and
judgmental schoolmates, into the pages and company of
adults who saw me as a peer rather than a flighty teen. They
loved my writing—I secreted their praise away like treasure.

They were too polite to say anything when, after he
returned, I stopped writing about our family and went
back to calling him Dad. I guess I decided to shelve my hurt
and direct my energies towards stories about living in the
city and running the store, where Hamilton, rather than
the members of my family, became the protagonist. And
I wrote as much for my monthly appointment at Duster's
as I did for myself. Good friends find ways to move around
grief and anger, so I fed the Guild as best I could, about
myself and what I loved, dressed up in stories and essays,
sometimes embellished, sometimes not.

I walked to the back of the bar to find the group waiting,
uncharacteristically punctual. They'd heard about the
robbery and wanted more details. All the regulars were
there. Eleanor sat at the head of the pulled-together tables
with her binders and notebooks. Marvin, a retired steel-
worker who churned out thriller stories, scratched his white
beard and winked at me as I sat. Theo peeked over the lid of
his laptop and then ducked back into his latest fantasy tale.
Sara's mouth moved rhythmically, silently reading through
one of her indecipherable poems. Bart was shaking his head
and grumbling about how angry the afternoon crowd had
been about the traffic disruption.

— You shoulda heard the white collars, he snorted. You'd think their world had ended.

— You'd think they'd have a little sympathy after a robbery, Eleanor agreed.

— Ach, you know how people get when they get something in their heads, he replied.

— How's your family doing, Mutton?

I shrugged and smiled, not wanting to get into it but not wanting to hurt Eleanor's feelings either. With most things, I was happy to share, but the robbery and my brother's injury were still tender points, even though I still had trouble remembering specifics. As a distraction I shuffled through the pages of Bart's latest story, another gory tale of zombies and vampires—or maybe a hybrid of the two, it was hard to tell—running havoc through Hamilton's core. Bart was Duster's short-order cook and he, although technically on the clock, never missed an opportunity to ply us with the macabre.

— Why are the stories always in Hamilton? You could set them anywhere, Eleanor said.

— Gotta get the fucking city on the map.

— Bart, language—

— Oh, come on—we're all grown-ups here.

— I'm not sure I see how vampires will make a difference, Marvin said.

— *Local* vampires, Bart said.

That started a lighthearted debate between the other members I couldn't find the energy to join. I watched the dusty ceiling fans spin lazy circles, wafting just enough air to stir the cobwebs between the rafters but do little at ground level. I dug for my phone and lost myself in a backlog of texts Peter had sent since leaving Leich and me in the store that morning. It was a play-by-play of what he'd been up to, people he'd seen, snacks he'd eaten. All to distract me. I smiled.

The Guild had gone silent, as though holding their collective breath. I snapped back to the present, heat flushing me from collar to hairline. I started to apologize.

— Sweetie, don't, Eleanor said. You're allowed to step away from reality every now and again, especially after what happened.

There were murmurs of agreement around the table.

— Thanks, I said.

— How's your story going? Marvin asked. Last meeting you said you'd have some ideas to run by us.

I hadn't gone any further than the fragmented brainstorming I'd told them about at the previous meeting.

— Fine, I said. I just left it at home.

— Next time, maybe, Theo said.

— Sure. Next time.

Why did I lie? I could have brought my notebook along. It was the first time since that nervous first meeting that I didn't have anything for the group to critique. I prided myself on being one of the more prolific contributors. But it was more than that; I loved sharing with them, using my writing as a way of letting things out, describing my life without describing my life. I knew that they too looked forward to stories I brought with me.

A few years before, in one of her moods, Mom had dismissed my writing as a hobby, something to be enjoyed but not pursued. She said it offhandedly like parents do when they're distracted, and I don't think she meant it. But over time, collecting her dismissals became as easy as collecting discarded coins on the sidewalk: there were lots of them when you started paying attention. Of course, my resolve to pursue writing as a career only strengthened—warn me about forbidden fruit and I'll just make a deeper study of every tree I pass.

The Guild had heard me talk about Toronto and journalism school, and making a living as a writer with dreams that travelled beyond Hamilton and our spot at Hughson and King. I suppose their support was the real draw for me to walk across Gore Park the day after the robbery. I might have outlined and character-sketched and brainstormed but my notebook hadn't moved from its place under the cash register in the store since before the robbery. My writer's brain recognized that my returning memories would bring reams of new material to share, but my heart hadn't let me pick up my pen. I wanted to come across the park, but carrying just myself.

— Eleanor, how do you—?

I stopped, torn between trust and the desire to protect my own privacy. I wanted to ask her how you move forward when you feel stuck, but balked. She looked over the rim of her glasses and searched me with a long look. And read my mind.

— One breath at a time, she said.

— Keep talking about it, Sara said.

— Keep writing, Bart chimed in.

Marvin and Theo grunted their agreement.

— About vampires and zombies, maybe, Bart said. Or both.

Eleanor threw a pretzel at him and missed.

It felt good to laugh.

A few mornings later, I decided to have my breakfast at the bottom of our apartment stairs, which I loved to do when the weather got warm. I'd sit with my cereal and orange juice and watch the city shift towards the working hours from my place on the stoop, cool in the shadows of the trees in the park and buildings across the street. The space warmed quickly, though, unprotected from the rising sun by the stubby green awning overhead.

When Dad bought the building, there were three tiny apartments upstairs, one above each store, built to accommodate the proprietors and their families. Instead of cramming us into one of those minuscule spaces, he knocked down a few walls and turned three apartments into one large one. At one end, our living room wall butted up against the cavernous, two-story space of City Bingo; at the other, our bedrooms always smelled of cooking oil from the various restaurants that opened and closed in the rental spaces next door. Our classy joint, Dad called it. He put up a long canvas and steel awning as a nod to New York City where, he said, all the best buildings had them. Within a few days, though, the bylaw people came by and ordered it cut back to a couple feet of overhang. I guess the idea of a sheltered dash to the curb didn't mesh with the wide, clear sidewalks the urban planners in our city had envisioned.

You can feel pretty possessive about a place. I thought of the stoop as my spot, where I could keep an eye on the neighbourhood. The weathered, historical facade of our building, the Weston Arcade, stretched east along the north side of King at Hughson. From where I sat, with my butt on the tiled floor of the landing and my slippered feet on the grimy concrete sidewalk, I had a good view. To my right, City Bingo and Second Chances; to my left, Razza's and Luigi's. Across the street was Gore Park, a thin, three-block wedge of urban green space with various statues, plaques, benches, and an obligatory fountain at the west end. The city always chose windy days to turn it on, making it impossible to sit anywhere nearby without a thorough misting. Duster's sat directly across the park, surrounded by a couple of grimy restaurants and empty storefronts.

But that morning, my mind was anywhere but on watching my neighbourhood. Just the day before, Razza's, a head shop that specialized in dated black T-shirts and water pipes, had served notice to my father that it was going out of business. Luigi's, an old-school tobacconist that had been forced to expand its offerings to include lottery tickets and porn rentals, had served its notice a few weeks earlier. You don't think much about the place you live while you're growing up there, but buying the Weston had been a risky move for my father. He was wealthy enough, having worked as a lawyer for a long time at one of the city's most trusted firms, but still needed the rental income from his tenants. He liked to say that he bought the old arcade for sentimental reasons and its architectural significance, but we knew it was so my mother could live her dream of running her own store.

Mom had lost her cool when Razza—a tall, lanky Barbadian with a bud-stained smile and dreadlocks—stopped by the store with a white legal envelope under his arm. He kept his eyes glued to the floor as he explained that he was closing and declaring bankruptcy. When he held out the envelope and asked her to give the letter to my father, she ripped it from his hands and yelled at him. He tried to apologize a bunch of times but she wouldn't let him finish, at one point smacking him on the arm with the envelope, making him flinch in retreat from the store. She'd been no kinder to my father and laid into him as soon as he got home from work, even though it was obvious he had no clue what she was so upset about. She stood over him and carried on as he opened the envelope, forcing him to try to read Razza's letter in the middle of her firestorm. The rest of the night was a blur of arguments and yelling and my mother dropping into desperate sessions of weeping. I went to bed at some point and tossed and turned, too wound up, falling into a fitful sleep well after midnight. An early streetside breakfast felt like just the thing to slough off the tension.

There was a banging sound to my left. A guy in dingy jeans and a beat-up leather jacket pounded against the glass in front of Luigi's and then leaned in drunkenly, trying to see through the dirty windows by cupping his hands around his face.

— Luigi's is closed? Shit, I wonder when that happened.

I recognized the leather jacket and the slurred voice. Bart wore it everywhere, no matter how hot or cold it was, because he said it reminded him of better times. He drank to battle the depression that being laid off from the steel mill had brought. He pulled a couple of shifts a week at Duster's so he could keep collecting his meagre welfare cheques.

He noticed me as he stepped away from the glass.

— Mutton, he said, and stumbled over.

— Hey, Bart.

He squinted at our storefront, weaving slightly on his feet.

— Where's the yellow police tape?

— We opened the day after the robbery.

— Oh.

I never asked him how old he was, but suspected the number was lower than I would have guessed. His shoulders were stooped, his legs bowed, his long, thin arms always folded, even when he walked, as though he was trying to hold himself together. And his hands were mill hands, perpetually chapped and rough. There were a lot of people like him in our city, especially as you went east from the downtown, a lot of people who hadn't moved well with the times. A lot of men with folded arms and old jackets.

— That's too soon, he said.

— What do you mean?

— Always wanting to move on after the bad things happen.

— What things?

— People get hurt. Bound to happen—stupid to open a store down here.

Bart shook his head and gave the store a dark look, then lightened his gaze when he looked at me. Then dark again. Bipolar almost, like hitting the switch in a too-bright room only to be bathed in dark you weren't quite ready for. I could have said something, but it's easier to let drunks ramble.

He looked at the sidewalk and shook his head again.

— Ah, shit, I'm sorry, Mutton. I love you guys, you know that, right?

— Sure do.

He held up his hand in a sort-of wave, then turned towards James Street, running his hand across the store windows and streaking the glass. I watched him go, concerned but not worried. God looking out for drunks and babies and whatnot. I smiled to myself, scooped the final bits of cereal into my mouth, and laid the bowl on the stoop. There is a kind of pride when you know your neighbourhood that well, even when it can change a man who writes vampire stories with the glee of a child into one who drinks so much he forgets that the sun will still rise the next day.

He'd never have said those things to Mom, of course. Not many people would. Maybe he was merely being perceptive, in his own way, about the kinds of emotions a mother would experience after having her children robbed at gunpoint. She hadn't been doing so well. Me neither. I was waking up a lot after dreams of guns and black holes. Leich continued to put on a brave face but the dark circles under his eyes made me want to ask if he was seeing what I was. Mom and Dad were short with each other. Even Wu was smiling less than normal.

Mr. Ahmad—he insisted we call him that—pulled his food cart onto the concrete pad at the east end of the park. He saw me, smiled, and waved. I returned the gesture and then gave in to a pleasant, zoned-out state where thinking and worrying weren't required, watching him get set up for the day. A few minutes later, footsteps on the hardwood stairs behind me brought me back to the present. My mother stepped past me and onto the sidewalk, pulling out her keys.

— Make sure those dishes get brought up to the apartment, Mutton.
— No one's ever stepped on them.
— I'm tired of dealing with dried cereal and dirty juice glasses every morning.

There was a flatness to her voice, as though she was passing along instructions to a computer rather than rebuking her daughter. Her clothes, always comfortable but well-fitted to her thin frame, seemed to hang like sackcloth, although that might have just been my lack of sleep. She had chosen a red shirt and tried to hide the fatigue, but the bright colour and the pale foundation looked even more garish as a result, like she was being held together by clown makeup.

I sighed and brought the dishes upstairs, dropping them into the sink to maximize the sound. By the time I went back down, she had moved in front of the store, frowning across the street at Mr. Ahmad as he lined up his drink selection along the edge of the cart.

— Why does he have to set up right there every day? That cart's an eyesore, she said, turning and putting the key in the lock.

She knew that he had paid for the permit to vend at that spot and that he wasn't going anywhere. Even I knew that. But right then probably wasn't the time to bring that up, so I just followed her into Second Chances, dragging my feet. I was scheduled to run things, but Mom had asked Leich to watch Wu so she could tidy things up in the back of the store. It would be just her and me in the store all day.

Have you ever missed someone who is still right in front of you? I missed my mother. Where was the old hippie, sunshine and light, happy to dispense unsolicited organic medical advice along with Second Chances' second-hand stuff? The one who looked forward to the Niche's daily offerings as much as Leich and I did? It was like life had become fine sandpaper, and she hadn't noticed the abrasion until it had worn through the skin and drawn blood. It wasn't just the money—she was happy to break even while Dad paid for the regular expenses—she probably saw the closing of Razza's and Luigi's as a loss of something bigger than rent revenue. Solidarity, perhaps, like they were in a good fight together. The terror of her kids being robbed while working in her downtown store. Wu's sickness worsening the abrasion.

She came out of the back room with that day's Niche offering, a heavy-looking, tarnished candlestick, and put it on a shelf without making sure it would fit. It ended up half on, half off an antique drink coaster and leaned precariously into the aisle. She was distracted, like she hoped her shadow might take care of the chores that needed doing. She even averted her eyes and took an extra step to the side as she passed the bullet hole as if they had the same polarity and were pushing away from each other.

— Should I get out the silver polish? I asked.

— It'll just get sold today anyhow.

The cash register drawer, which had been left open overnight, stuck its black tongue at me as a reminder about the float.

— Mom, how about the cash?

No response. I started towards the back to get it from the safe. Mom brushed by me to grab a dirty rag from under the counter and went to clean the door window. I stopped and watched her push the grime around in circles as she stared at King, not noticing that she was making more work for herself.

No, she wasn't herself. This was not the woman who named her children on whims, saying that life was too short to spend too much time on single decisions. She actually thought Mutton was an elegant choice for a squalling baby girl, a notion no one else seemed to share.

She thought Leich sounded nice in its native German and so she dropped it on her firstborn, unaware that everyone on this side of the Atlantic would have trouble pronouncing it. Wu was the name of a favourite Chinese takeout place that had gone under, so she resurrected the name and laid it on their post-reunion lovechild. When I asked her why she'd chosen my name, she told me to say it with punch, holding it behind my teeth, and I'd understand. I never did. She left us to deal with the funny looks and thoughtless comments—Wow, you must hate that!—and never looked back. We hadn't made too big a deal about them, though. A funny thing about names, even strange or bad or bizarre ones: how completely they can weld themselves to a person.

At the safe, I counted out the bills and change and walked back to the front, sliding the cash tray into the register drawer, which took its customary two attempts to close. So familiar, yet it called to mind the memory of Leich bleeding as he slumped against the wall. My breath caught and I steadied myself against the counter, noticing that the sepia photograph, its glass starred with cracks, still leaned against the baseboard behind the counter. Worried about Wu's wandering hands, I picked it up, the cracks grinding, loud against the morning quiet, and slid it onto a shelf under the till.

Mom came back, stuffed the rag under the counter, and sat on the old black vinyl barstool behind the till, trapping me between her and the front display window. Her eyes closed as soon as she sat and she didn't move for what seemed like a full minute, even though it was probably only a few seconds.

— Mom? The window?

— Sure, honey.

— What?

40

— No, that's all right.

I groaned as I took the rag, squeezed myself between her and the wall, and walked around the counter and to the filthy front door.

— Morning, King Street, I said under my breath.

— Just open the doors, Mutton, Mom said. Let's get some fresh air in here.

— But we never leave the door open. What if—

— We'll be fine.

Still that robotic tone. She hadn't moved and her eyes were still closed. Another pang of memory dug into my diaphragm, but she was right—it wasn't the open door that brought the robber in. I opened Second Chances to the sounds of cars and trucks and buses and a city resolving itself to another day. There was no wind apart from the air pushed aside by the traffic; the smell of the steel mills hung low to the ground.

— It is good that you are open again!

— Shit! I said, startled.

The voice belonged to The Outfit, someone I hadn't seen in quite some time, someone I would like never to have seen in the first place. His accent was Eastern European, and he was always proper when he spoke, exceedingly polite. He was a local real estate developer known for the investments he had made in the city, and he wanted the Weston. It was as simple as that. Dad had declined the The Outfit's various offers, saying that they sounded too sweet to be real sugar. The Outfit had a reputation for smooth-talking his way into deals by promising the sun, only to hide behind his lawyers as he demolished building after building, leaving the owners, tenants, and residents without umbrellas for the inevitable rain. Dad had told him firmly that he wouldn't sell, even as the other shops faded away. And no one had inquired about renting the vacant spaces, which meant that The Outfit was exerting pressure we couldn't see. The timing of his visit, so soon after Razza and Luigi gave notice was of course predictable to the point of cliché.

He had impeccable taste in clothing, so I'd given him the nickname The Outfit. I had tried a few different nicknames, but they were either too obvious or too profane to use in everyday conversation. Leich said I put too much mental effort into my nicknames, but it gave me something to do with the identities of the people I didn't—or thought I wouldn't—like. No one needed to know that it was a much preferred, constructive diversion from a mental instinct I'd trained myself to internalize, which was to classify things formally. Last name, first name. The pattern worked for situations, too, or places. Or anything, really, as long as I switched the syntactical order around and inserted a comma. Possible alternative to The Outfit?

Asshole, Arrogant.

As my heart rate returned to normal, The Outfit frowned like he was either disappointed by my unlady-like language or that I'd frightened so easily. But then his expression changed to concern so quickly I almost expect-ed to hear a clicking sound.

— I was grieved to hear of the robbery and what happened to your brother.

— Thank you, I said.

A reflexive expression of thanks—I had few illusions about how bad he really felt.

He was a mobster. Many of the developers in the core were. In terms of business and economic aspirations, we lived in a young city with industrial roots, where it was easy for corruption to grease this and nudge that, the certainty of money in palms an easier sell than patience and progress. The Outfit was no exception, yet even at my age I could tell that he was playing a longer game. That he would arrive first thing in the morning looking as crisp as a new hundred-dollar bill, while most of the gangsters were still sleeping, said a lot. His suits— he always wore suits—were finely tailored and looked expensive, and I never saw a single scuff mark on his shoes, not ever. No ostentatious jewelry, either, just a simple watch on a leather band and a plain wedding ring. Manicured hands. Fantastic ties. Yes, I loved his ties, always the perfect shade and knot. I had, at one point, thought about calling him The Tie, but decided not to diminish them by association.

Despite his apparent attention to the finer things, though, you couldn't say he was anything other than a hard man. His elegance merely accentuated his sharpness, like a straight razor sheathed in silk used to cut someone's throat. Such refinement and edge that you might even forget how short he was, standing five-foot-nothing at most.

— Is your father in?

A frightening question, I have no trouble admitting, just by how normal it was.

— No, just Mom.

His unlined, blemish-free face brightened.

— That is excellent! I have not seen Anne in ages. May I come in, please?

Do you see what I mean? He was perfect, just perfect. Even the most everyday questions were weighted so you had no choice other than to agree. Would I, a fifteen-year-old shopkeeper's daughter who knew all about the man, even think about saying no? Of course not.

— Please, after you, my dear.

The next thing I knew he was chivalrously gesturing me inside and I was leading him in to see my mother. Lambs and butchers, maybe. An expensive black sedan pulled up to the curb and stopped right in the no parking zone, its four-ways flashing. Angry drivers slammed on the brakes, wheeled around, and laid on their horns. The two large men sitting in the front seats looked forward impassively. The Outfit saw the car, looked at his watch, and shook his head as he stopped in front of the cash register and my mother.

— I am sorry for this. They were to wait until I called.

My mother opened her eyes and tilted her head at him, skeptical. No, her eyes seemed to say, the guys came precisely as arranged. Message received.

He looked around the shop, his eyes resting on the uneven white patch where the bullet hole had been. I'd walked in the day before to find Mom on the stepladder, putty knife in hand, defiantly covering over the hole with drywall compound. They took pictures, she'd said. Why should I wait months and months for trial, when they haven't found the guy and probably never will? The rough, unpainted repair stood out, like our walls had developed a mild case of vitiligo.

— It is sad when the young ones resort to such methods, you would agree, The Outfit said.

— Michael isn't here.

— So your daughter tells me. It is no problem—I have his cell number. But now that I am here, maybe I can speak with you.

— We're not selling.

— *We*, you say, but this is not the case.

— I think we've—he's—made it clear that—

— Clear, yes, but there are always ways—no, this is the wrong word—discussions that can be had.

My mother shifted forward, her eyes blazing. Is it wrong to admit that, as he let the unsaid hang in the air like a foul smell, seeing my mother's spark return made me glad? Just as she was about to reply—with something distinctly un-organic, I was sure—a woman came in, dragging the street noise with her. She was dressed in a light grey suit, unbuttoned to reveal a cream blouse, a large purse slung across her chest. There was redness high on her cheeks, like she had been walking for some time. She greeted the three of us with a cheerful hello, clueless to the tension that had been building, and began to browse.

— Anne, Anne, I think that perhaps—

— You should leave, Mom said. I have a customer.

The Outfit sniffed as Mom turned towards the woman in the store, who wasn't aware of being observed. When the woman happened upon the silver candlestick, a squeak of joy escaped her lips. She looked under the base for the price tag but, finding none, frowned briefly before holding it up and calling out.

— How much for the candlestick?

She'd modulated her voice into a more businesslike tone. The best second-hand shoppers love to find items without price tags as much as an archaeologist loves to find cave paintings or old bones. Of course, we had witnessed her excitement, and less scrupulous vendors would have overcharged her. One of the things we never did for Niche items was overcharge, knowing somehow that to do so would be an insult least of all to the shopper, most of all to the universe. Mom pretended to think about it before telling her she could have it for five dollars. The woman smiled, clasped the candlestick to her chest, and came to the register.

The Outfit watched her. When she placed the candlestick on the counter to dig out her wallet, his eyes narrowed and he licked his upper lip like he'd noticed a bit of caviar he'd missed on his dinner plate. I half expected him to salivate.

— I must be going now, but thank you for inviting me in, he said. Do pass along my best to your husband and your two boys.

My mother didn't respond. I certainly didn't know what to say.

— Thank you so much, this is perfect, the woman said. How long have you been in business?

This was one of my mother's favourite questions, so I waited for her usual answer; she savoured the tally a little more each time. But she hadn't heard the woman, and simply glared at The Outfit in silence.

— Uh, a while, I said.

— I never even knew you were here. I just had this feeling.

She tucked her wallet and the candlestick into her purse before moving towards the door. The Outfit moved smoothly past her.

— Please, allow me.

— So gallant. I guess chivalry isn't dead, she said, laughing.

Mom took a huge breath—had she been holding it the whole time?—as the two of them walked out onto the sidewalk. Then she leaned back and again closed her eyes, her hands resting on her lap in tight little fists.

A short while later, I found myself wandering up James Street North, towards the harbour.

Still seething at The Outfit's intrusion, Mom had kicked me out, saying she needed to be alone. Her strength throughout the encounter had been impressive and I had just resolved to be a more accommodating companion when she dismissed me.

— I can help, I said.

— I'll take care of everything, she said.

— But—

— Just go.

She hurt my feelings. That wasn't her intent, but it still stung, especially the residual heat in her voice, hot coals burned down to grey.

I didn't storm out, but I didn't leave quietly either. The prospect of carte blanche to disappear for the rest of the day overruled my wounds enough to ask for some money. Mom rang open the till and handed over a twenty-dollar bill without a word. I could have gone back upstairs and just grabbed my wallet and my satchel but it felt good to reclaim a fleeting mote of control. Besides, Leich would have dragged the story out of me and I didn't feel like reliving it, nor did I relish the melodramatic guilt trip he would inevitably lay about being stuck with Wu while I got to do whatever I wanted.

My eventual destination was Bayfront Park, a green spit of land that thrust into Hamilton Harbour, to try and do some writing on one of the benches that faced the water. It was a long but pleasant walk, particularly along James, where I could peek into the windows of some of the city's other thrift stores and the art galleries that seemed to be cropping up all over. My abrupt departure necessitated a stop at Zim's, an art supply store that carried my favourite brand of notebooks and pens. The owner, an old Frenchman named Paul, had the remarkable ability never to forget a face or a name, greeting his customers in an accent as smoky as a Paris café. It's nice to be recognized, sometimes.

I crossed Gooseberry Street and walked past the coffee-house perched on the corner. Bright days can sometimes turn windows into mirrors, and I noticed a dark smudge under my left eye as I passed by. I stopped, leaned in to see myself more clearly and wiped it away—it looked like the grease a baseball player of old might use to reduce the sun's glare, but I couldn't imagine where I had picked it up.

My outline in the streak-free window revealed more and more of the shop's interior. I didn't feel as awkward as I should have, the looming teenager looking through the glass, intruding into the customers' quiet morning. A movement caught my eye. A man in a suit leaned back and laughed, touching the arm of his companion, a petite brunette with her back to the window. Then he saw me, and saw that I saw him, and his laughter faded. The woman turned to see what had caused him to pause, and I saw her face, pale, her dark hair in a loose updo, her lipstick subdued.

She was stunning. And leaning over a table with my father. In the middle of the work day. I found a label to file her under.

Mistress, Beautiful.

I stepped back, my reflection shrinking, the brightness of the street eclipsing the portal through which I'd seen my father laughing and touching that woman.

— Hey! Watch it!

I nearly collided with a grungy-looking street punk decked out in tattoos and piercings and a rigid, finlike mohawk. I muttered an apology and fled north, away from the shop. I didn't see the fire hydrant, which pranged into my shin, causing me to stumble.

— Mutton, wait!

My father's voice, behind. I tried to keep moving, but the bright stars of pain in my shin made me limp. Then he was beside me, holding me up, asking if I was all right. No, Michael, I'm not all right, I thought. Would you be, having seen what I just saw, having lived through what we all lived, having forgiven what we'd forgiven?

— Come back inside. You need to sit down.

— Is she all right? Here, let me help.

Even her voice was lovely. She put her arms around my shoulders, the gentle scent of her expensive perfume carrying me back into the coffee shop. They sat me at the table as Dad barked at the barista for some ice. Dad's companion fussed over me and dragged a chair over just for my leg. I felt nauseated from the pain, which had inserted itself into the centre of my shin, and from the tightness in my stomach, clenched like a fist. All of the questions you can imagine were a rolling boil inside, but nothing came out. The ice arrived and was laid, angular and hard, on the rising lump on my shin. Barely cool through my jeans.

A long moment passed, suspended between uncertainty and discomfort. The woman patted me on the shoulder and rustled together the folders and papers from her side of the table. There were abbreviated words of farewell between her and my father. My shin pain gave way to a needy numbness. I felt trails of wetness move down my cheeks, cooled by the conditioned air.

He spoke first.

— God, that had to hurt. Does your leg feel better?

— Dad, who is she?

— You ran into that hydrant full tilt.

— Does Mom know?

He sat back, eyebrows pinched. Then he closed his eyes and sighed, his understanding moving beyond concern for his injured daughter. He loosened his tie and undid the top button of his shirt.

— She's a colleague—a *former* colleague—from the office. You've met her, actually.

Had I? I couldn't recall. Then I saw the table, covered by booklets and papers. His favourite pen, expensive, always the last thing he grabbed after his keys and wallet and phone, slid precisely into his shirt pocket before saying his goodbyes for the day, resting atop a number of thick legal folders. His briefcase sat on the floor, vertical, ready for action.

A business meeting. Stupid.

— I'm sorry, Dad. I just thought—

He smiled a little, still uncomfortable, and brought his hand to his forehead, rubbing it like he was trying to wipe something away.

— That's all right. I'm sorry you were so startled. You're going to have quite a bruise.

He sat forward and reached for his mug of coffee. He took a sip, his eyes fixed firmly on the work materials strewn across the table. It must have been some meeting, I thought. There was just so much stuff.

— Can I get you something to drink?

— Some juice, maybe.

He put the mug down, signalled the barista to come over, and started gathering the folders and papers together. He made some small talk, asking what I was up to and so on, as the juice was placed in front of me. A few of the thinner items went into the briefcase. Just as I was thinking of the best way to bring up The Outfit's visit, he leaned over and tucked the larger folders in a cardboard banker's box on the floor, wedged between his chair and the wall. That has to be heavy, I thought, noting how far we were from his office. It didn't mean anything that I'd never seen him at the shop before, but his tailored suit and crisp tie were a marked contrast from what the other patrons were wearing. And that box, it was like he had brought his office with him. He had a corner office with an amazing view of the north city, and there were a number of upscale coffee shops nearer to his building. Why come here at all?

He saw me look at the box.

— You don't miss much, do you?

I opened my mouth and closed it again.

— I lost my job a few weeks ago.

— What? Dad, how—?

— Hard times, they said.

— But you've been there for so long, how can they just fire you?

— It's more complicated than that.

— What about your clients? The business you brought in?

— They're not mine, not really.

— So you just—

— I've been working out of coffee shops, trying to get enough work together to start again on my own.

— What about her? I nodded at the door.

— She—Sylvia—meets me here and floats me overflow business the firm can't take.

— So she's just a—

— She could lose her job if anyone knew.

— Mom doesn't know.

— I haven't told her yet, no.

He deflated as he said it.

51

— I'm trying to find the right opportunity.

— Dad, you have to.

— I'm sorry, Mutton. I wanted to carry this one on my own.

I told him about The Outfit's visit and how strong Mom had been, how her strength came from Dad's refusal to give in, his resolve to do the right thing. My own strength pushed forward, too, in strange solidarity with my mother despite that morning's disappointment.

— You have to tell her soon, Dad. If you don't—

— I know. Can you give me a few days? I'd understand if you can't.

— I guess.

No assumption, no leverage, no effort to manipulate, just a defeated expression and a genuine request to let him try, even with the knowledge of how unfair his request was. Still, my father's dishonesty—or perhaps his *less*-than honesty, given that he had confided in me when he had to—nagged as I limped away from the café, thinking about the various kinds of bruises that bloom when you walk into something unexpected.

P eter was waiting on the sidewalk for me when I came down from the apartment. He had texted the night before to ask if I'd be interested in an outing—yes, he actually used the word outing. He wouldn't give me any more details, which annoyed me, but since spontaneity was a rare thing for him, I agreed. And I needed to get out, having had plenty of time to weigh the ramifications of Dad losing his job, which went well beyond not telling Mom. How much work could a lawyer solicit from a coffee shop table? How long did we have before the financial issues became unavoidable? Was he all right? I had finally fallen asleep only to find myself immersed in dreams of homelessness and family strife, where we abandoned each other in our own search for survival, feral and lost.

— You're limping, he said.

— Oh, right. That. Banged my shin on a fire hydrant yesterday.

— Are you all right? Can I—

My hand came up flapping, waving away his concern like it was nothing, cutting him off. I started to walk away but Peter stayed put, forcing me to stop and go back a few steps.

— Maybe we should do this another time, he said.

— *Do* what exactly?

His eyebrows moved up and down, perplexed.

— Well, it's a surprise, but I can look into rescheduling.

— I'll be fine, I said. Let's just go.

— You sure?

— Yes.

— All right.

I was foul, no doubt about it, but in an unsolvable way, like I'd attracted a swarm of gnats. I just had to put up with it, like Peter so often chose to put up with me. He and I had become best friends at school, on the first day of Grade Nine, the year before. The closure of some of the old schools across the city and the construction of newer, bigger buildings had forced a bunch of students into new districts. I would've had to go to the crumbling old school in the north end, but they turned that one into a technical school so I was shunted into a new building tucked against the escarpment south of downtown. We were assigned to the same homeroom and gravitated together when we realized that everyone else knew each other, protected by that invisible force field of loyalty carried into one's teenage years. Mind you, I had seen Peter walking down the hall in his chinos and beige linen shirt—what Grade Nine boy dresses like that?—and had decided not to like him. By the time we got to homeroom, I had christened him The Beige. Naturally, the only open seat was right next to him, so I tried to avert my gaze as I sat down. He smiled and started talking to me—actually, he was so at ease it was more like he was picking up an old conversation than starting a new one. The homeroom teacher, who arrived a few minutes late, had to ask us directly to stop chatting; I hadn't noticed that Peter and I had been talking at all, so quickly we fell into each other's rhythms.

— So, are you going to tell me where we're headed?

— You'll see.

Despite my grumpiness, he'd regained some of his excitement. He handed over a small green card with a flourish.

— For you, my dear, he said. Transit card. Pre-loaded.

Intriguing, I thought.

Then he turned away, blushing into his collar. Peter had an interesting sense of fashion, a mishmash of styles, like he had gone to the mall and sampled a bit from every store. The one constant was his absolute adherence to a colour palette of earth tones. When he wore a baseball hat, for example, even the stitching had to be green or brown. That morning, he was wearing baggy chinos and a faded green polo, which told me nothing: he could have been planning a trip to church or the park or to the theatre.

I wanted to tell him about Dad, just to have an outlet and maybe some support, but I didn't; my promise had been half-hearted, but still a promise. Yet not telling Peter felt strange—I told him everything. We crossed Hughson and waited for the lights to cross King, my mind jumping between my father's dilemma and today's adventure. The light changed, and we walked—with me trying to hide my limp—into the park, where Mr. Ahmad was leaning against his cart with his face towards the sun.

— Hi, Mr. Ahmad, I said.

He looked down at us and grinned.

— Miss Mutton and Mr. Peter, he said. Good morning to you.

— How's business? Peter asked.

— It will be a good day, Mr. Ahmad said. Like yesterday and the day before.

You had to admire the man's optimism. He did a fair business with the lunchtime crowd, dispensing falafel and shawarma with good cheer and tons of garlic to the worker drones buzzing out from their hives for thirty minutes of midday freedom. He had two dreams: his first was to put his children through university; his second to bring breakfast falafel to the people of our city. So he set up his cart early, even on weekends, in the hope that people would discover and then crave his homemade falafel recipe.

My mother could never get over the name of his business—Satan's Falafel—but I enjoyed having him around. She particularly chafed at the sign atop his cart, yellow capital letters on a red background screaming SATAN'S FALAFEL amidst the park's more subdued stones and trees. Ever since he obtained permission to set up on the fountain side of the park, there'd been fewer incidents and fights and less all-around grunginess in the green centre of our city, which used to be ground zero for the city's homeless and unsavoury characters. He told me once where the name came from, the story involving an irritable immigration official, a misheard translation of one of his given names, and an incorrectly completed form. His name, of course, had not even a trace of Satan in it, but he loved the story, saying it was one of his first true immigration experiences, that his cart should be a tribute to the great nation that had allowed him to start over again. Even a legal challenge by The Shirt, our ward councilman over at city hall, had been thrown out of court by a judge who said that using an unfortunate name didn't make it illegal.

Mr. Ahmad turned serious and looked me in the eye.

— You and your brother are all right?

— We are, thanks for asking.

— Good. That is good. Breakfast?

Peter and I looked at each other and shrugged—his food was delicious, but I'd never had it for breakfast—and said okay. He grabbed two fresh sub rolls and loaded them up with the greenish falafel, tahini, lettuce, tomato, and cucumber, and a couple of thick-cut french fries, wrapping each heaping sandwich in a perfect length of foil. Peter tried to pull out his wallet, but Mr. Ahmad playfully threatened him with the fork he had used to crush the falafel balls.

— Is on my house today, he said.

We thanked him and walked south towards Main Street, which ran as busily to the east as King did to the west. At the bus stop, Peter checked the schedule on his phone and declared that we would have time to eat our falafels before the bus arrived. They were delicious, enough so to ignore the dragon-breath we'd undoubtedly have for the rest of the day. We ate in comfortable silence and he looked pleased with himself, enjoying his role as the day's organizer.

Peter kept the secret all the way to the northeast end of the city, where the bus hissed and belched us out onto a cracked sidewalk. People said that this end of town always lived in the shadows of the mills which, in the old days, was a literal shadow in the form of the smog that poured out from the smelters and coke ovens. Although environmental regulations had curbed the emissions from the remaining two mills, you could still see the rusted, shuttered plants and mills from almost every street in the east end of the city. You felt the shadow in other ways. Pensioners walked a little less straight, coughed a little more. Roads were repaired less often. Old grime persisted under eaves and overhangs where the rain couldn't wash it away.

Occasionally, though, there were glimpses of light that bathed this end of the city in its steel-town heyday. Once, Dad told me never to underestimate those who took on hard industry, that their spines and wills were fused not only to the products they made but their employers and unions too. Even Bart, who slung burgers and fries at a downtown bar for minimum wage and had been laid off from more industries than he could count, lit up when he talked about his industrial past. He'd shown me photos of family picnics held by the mill owners and snapshots of his father and grandfather posing with union-led bowling and softball teams. Here, too, I'd recognize that what Peter was about to show me was a way to reclaim some dignity and have some fun for people who can be forgotten when success moves elsewhere.

Peter pulled a colourful pamphlet from his back pocket.

— They're holding the fair on the old mill grounds, out near the plants themselves, he gushed.

— What fair?

— The pamphlet says it's for the mill families, but anyone can go.

One of his other quirks was his twin loves of architecture and the construction of precise models of Hamilton buildings. His current project was a scale replica of the Catholic cathedral that overlooked the west end of the city from its perch above the highway. He'd constructed everything by hand, right down to the pews and altars, and nothing brought him more pleasure than sitting down to whittle a piece of balsa wood into an architectural feature. While other guys his age were smoking pot and checking out girls on social media, he was getting buzzed by Googling online images of famous buildings and flirting with foam board and resin and model glue. An exaggeration? Maybe, but his father had been an architect who encouraged him to build things with the scraps of his own projects, his mother a children's book illustrator. Creating was in his genes.

When he was in Grade Seven, both of his parents were killed by a drunk driver at a Dundas stoplight, so he went to live with his aunt. She was a large person, literally and figuratively, so huge with goodness you'd want to follow her down the street just to see the smiles she brought to other people's faces. The first time we went to his place after school, she took one look at me and said I looked like a writer. Peter must have told her, I reasoned at the time, embarrassed by the attention. However, seeing how she nurtured Peter's gifts by meting out generous portions of his parents' life insurance payout for architectural modelling supplies, I think she just saw *me*. After that, I was pretty much her adopted second child.

A powerful thing, recognition; it can cover us in warmth as easily as strip us bare. Anyhow, Peter's the first to credit his present livelihood as a notable architect to the foresight of a big, loving aunt who believed in building him up rather than quashing his quirks. Everyone should be so fortunate.

We walked down Burlington Street and onto Industrial, where one of the mill's huge parking lots had been transformed into a fair, complete with rides, game stalls, vendors, and a small midway. It looked like someone had thrown brightly coloured paint all over, a burst of life against the rusty buildings and pipe jungles. The smell of the mills wasn't as strong here, surprisingly, leaving the carnies and fairgoers to breathe in the sun-warmed asphalt and savoury smells from the food tents.

— I wonder why they're holding it here, I said.

— I think there's a charity involved.

— No, I mean why have it in a parking lot next to a working mill? There are so many empty lots around.

— I like it. Feels more real, somehow.

At the gate, a handful of men wearing union hats and embroidered jackets took our entry fee and waved us in with shaky hands and grateful smiles. We walked around for a while, playing a couple of games, looking at the cheap trinkets and dusty crafts, and eating deep-fried Mars bars from a rusty American food truck. The turnout wasn't great; only a small number of families with squirrelly little ones milling around and other teenagers looking at their cell phones more than spending money.

— So are you going to tell me what's wrong, or do I have to guess?

We had stopped in front of a game stall, the one where you try to toss a softball into an extra-springy bushel the carnies modify so only a miracle will keep the ball in.

— What do you mean?

He grunted and shook his head.

— Always the closed book, eh?

— I'm not.

— You are. Of course, I know better.

Logically, there was no way he could have known, and yet his eyes looked so clear and intense I worried for a moment I had let Dad's secret slip. I tried to think through the various conversations we'd had. After a moment, I realized he was waiting for an answer.

— It's just—no, nothing's wrong. I'm fine. It'll be fine.

He folded his arms and tilted his head, skeptical as a priest, and waited. So did I, clenching my jaw to keep from telling him everything—that's how badly I craved his input. After a long beat, he sighed and walked away. I watched his shoulders tense as I caught up, but he didn't say anything. I knew the game. We walked in silence for a while. Eventually, he relaxed, and tilted his hat towards the back of the lot.

— Let's see how close we can get to the outbuildings, Peter said.

— I don't know—they've kept the fair far away for a reason, I think.

— We're not going to break in, or anything—I just want to get closer.

— All right.

He grinned.

We walked to the rear of the fair, where the carnies' trailers were guarded by a long row of blue porta-potties. Thick, greasy cables ran everywhere, between the buildings and under our feet. A number of generators chugged away behind the trailers, the sharp odour of diesel weaving between everything.

— Hey.

Peter and I whirled around, startled. The voice belonged to a guy leaning against the back of a trailer, his hands buried deep in his pockets.

— Either of you got an extra cigarette?

— Uh, no, Peter said. Don't smoke.

— Me, neither, I said.

— No problem. Thanks anyway.

As though he'd already forgotten about us, the guy closed his eyes and leaned his head back against the trailer's dented metal siding. He was about our age, maybe a year or two older, wearing a black shirt and jeans and all the right accessories: studded belt, Chucks, and a mop of limp hair that fell across one of his eyes. A frayed messenger bag cut a diagonal across his chest, and a pink and black striped scarf hung through the strap. The look reminded me of the dark phase Leich had gone through a year or two before. How moody my brother had been, slouching around, not talking to anyone, bringing a cloud of sadness wherever he went. Locked doors. Monosyllabic responses. Shrugs. You know. This guy, too, looked like a lot of boys in that phase, trying to be noticed through a wash of sameness. I filed him under Boy, Unimpressive, before cycling through a list of possible nicknames. Emo. The Chuck. The Sad. And so on.

— Let's get going, Peter said, interrupting my thoughts.

— Have fun, you two, the guy said, his eyes remaining closed.

He sounds like a parent, I thought as Peter and I walked away and started across the parking lot. Weird.

The lot was huge, with the fair—which we'd thought was sizeable—occupying only a small portion of it. The sounds of games and rides faded behind us as we crossed the expanse of lined asphalt, replaced by the mechanical sounds of the mills. The buildings and structures grew. I didn't say much as Peter pointed out the different buildings to me—coke ovens, blast furnaces, milling areas, continuous casting, rolling mills, and so on—letting him deliver a satisfied monologue.

— I'd love to build a scale model of this place someday, he said.

— That would take years, right?

I figured that so much time would have been a barrier. He didn't. He just smiled a dreamy smile, as though nothing could make him happier.

— Yeah, probably.

A massive bloom of bluish-orange flame erupted from a tall, thin structure I had assumed was a smokestack. Even from a few hundred feet away, we could feel the concussion in our chests and a brush of warmth against our faces.

Burnoff from one of the ovens, maybe. Peter laughed and began to run, hopping nimbly over some narrow-gauge tracks cutting across the pavement to get closer to the fence. My shin ached, so I had to follow more slowly. By the time I reached him, he had his fingers laced through the chain-link and was watching the fire and the buildings, smiling to burst. He looked up and down the fence line.

— Maybe we can sneak in, he said.

— That's not a good idea.

What I said was a reflex, a thing to fill space as my mind spun around my friend's law-breaking suggestion. A minor thing, to be sure—we were just fifteen after all, and how much could two of us do to a steel mill?—but it still shocked me into the rote response. He was serious, too, with a set jaw and a look in his eye that could have been mischief. I wasn't keen, but you back up your friends, so I played along, gamely scanning the fenceline even though it was at least eight feet high and was topped with razor wire. It was sound, no holes or breaks anywhere in sight. He looked disappointed. We stood in silence for a long while, the heat from the burnoff diminishing as the flame settled into itself, and listened to the mysterious rumbles and clangs and booms from inside the mill. Instinctively, my mind began making stories up for each one, a dropped crucible here, a steel slab there, workers forced to close the gargantuan doors of a runaway blast furnace.

He took out his phone and began taking photos of me against the fence with the mills as my backdrop.

— What are you doing?

— You had this look on your face, he said. So serious, but nice, too.

— Come on, knock it off.

He lowered the phone a tiny bit and looked at me with a strange expression. Expectant, almost. Eager.

— I'm glad you came today. I wanted to—

His voice gave out on him mid-sentence and his face erupted red. He got like that, sometimes, flustered when he couldn't find the right words, and I knew to give him space instead of trying to help. I waited, steadying myself against the fence with one hand and lightly rubbing my bruised shin with the other.

— You are—I mean—it means—

He stopped again, his cell still suspended between us like a microphone.

— Hey! You can't be here! No pictures!

We spun to face the voices. Two plant security guards— huge men with dark grey uniforms and frighteningly full belts—had driven up in a golf cart. They looked angry but at the same time satisfied with themselves for scaring us. Peter started to apologize and took a step towards the guards, forgetting about the steel rails embedded in the pavement. His shoe caught in the groove and he fell, his ankle popping audibly. He cried out in pain, rolling on the rough surface. Whatever space I'd created for him evaporated. I knelt as he held his ankle and groaned, trying to reassure him, my own shin barking, feeling about as useful as fingernail dirt.

In a blink, the guards' demeanour changed from bulldog to kitten, and they leapt from the cart, looking concerned and, to my satisfaction, maybe a little worried about having gone too far. One of them unclipped a radio and called for an ambulance. The crackled response was unintelligible. The guard with the radio, older than his colleague by a handful of grey hairs, asked which hospital they should bring Peter to.

At the mention of the word hospital, I remembered telling Leich I'd go with him to St. Joe's to get his stitches out. I checked the time on my phone and slapped myself on the forehead.

— Shit, I said.

— What? Peter asked through gritted teeth.

— Leich gets his stitches out today. Right now.

I turned on my phone, took a step away, and called my brother. The third ring cut out partway and went right to voicemail. I imagined him sitting in the cracked vinyl waiting room chairs and pulling out his phone, seeing my number on his screen, and pushing the big red button. My brother had declined my too-late, guilty call.

Mom brought Wu down to Second Chances so she could do paperwork. When they came in, he almost knocked my mother off balance as he reached for me across the counter. I took him, trying not to bang his knees on the counter, and hoisted him onto my own hip. He nuzzled into my neck. My mother smiled.

— He's all yours, she said.

— Thanks, I guess.

— You can bring him back when he starts to get crazy again.

When, not *if*. Wu giggled, as though he knew exactly how crazy he was prepared to get, and waved at Mom's back as she walked away. I scratched his back—another of his favourite things—making him wiggle against me, pleased as a puppy. In such moments, it was easy to forget how sick he was. You'd assume he was just another toddler looking for big sister cuddles, unaware that most kids his age were bigger than he was, that he should be shedding his toddler skin. He was too small, his body clashing against his exuberance and his mind, and it was far too easy to lift him like we did. Still, within a few minutes, he was squirming to be put down like any other boy, running to the back as soon as I set him onto his feet. I heard the squeak of the old office chair as my mother picked him up; in a moment I knew I'd hear another one when he fought to be put down again.

— That didn't take long, she called from the back. You couldn't keep him up there?

— I couldn't have kept him if I tried, Mom.

I went back to what I had been doing, which was pretending to read my favourite Miriam Toews novel. Days in the store were always slow so I read a lot, something everyone in the writer's group envied me for. Read a lot, write a lot, was the mantra. I consumed books like they were food and I was starving, particularly stories of quirky, rebellious females with odd names. I don't know how many copies of *A Boy of Good Breeding* I had, but they were everywhere, in all stages, from ratty and falling apart to a never-touched, autographed hardcover my mother had gotten for me. There was a backup copy under the till in the store, too, because I never knew when I might need a good fix of memorable characters.

But not that morning—there had been too many surprises lately, too many reasons not to lose myself in a story, mine or anyone's. Leich was supposed to be working, but my guilt—at missing his appointment on Saturday— volunteered me to take his shift. He didn't make a big deal of my absent-mindedness, thinking it would make me feel worse which, at any other time, would've been true. He savoured it, actually, accepting my peace offering with a noncommittal shrug betrayed by a glint in his eye. But my strategy was as much to have time to myself as it was an apology for leaving him alone while the doctor snipped the stitches, so I put on a performance of my own, enduring his little guilt trip as though there was nothing more I needed than to take his place in the store.

I hadn't anticipated, though, that there was such a thing as too much time to think. Dad hadn't told Mom yet, and I was starting to chafe from carrying the secret.

The door opened, bringing the comforting wash of traffic noise. In came Saul, a special-needs man from one of the group homes over on Victoria Street. He liked to sneak out and wander around the downtown. The home was notorious for forgetting about their tenants and we had brought Saul—a cheerful, mute man in his twenties with motor and movement challenges—back a few times. We hadn't seen him for months, though, because Leich had to call the police the last time after discovering him touching himself in our small curtained change room. He refused to leave, forcing staff from the home to bring specialized restraints. Mom had called the home and laid into the supervisor, telling him that Saul was banned from the premises.

— Saul, you can't be here, I said.

There was no indication that he'd heard me. We had instructions from his group home to call the police if he came back but I wasn't comfortable arresting or restraining someone who had no idea what he was doing. I dug out my phone to call the home instead and watched him shuffle slowly around the shop, occasionally stopping and staring at objects on the shelves.

I hesitated, seeing that he was holding the pen he had purchased from us a couple of years earlier. The pen, one of those heavy space pens that can write upside down and underwater, was a Niche item. Mom told us how Saul had just walked straight to it without looking at a single other item, how he'd paid with a pocketful of pennies and nickels and dimes. Stories like these cemented our relationship with the neighbourhood, so it was hard to make the call, knowing that even if the cops didn't come there was still likely to be unpleasantness. Still, the robbery was fresh and the thought of the unknown was enough to push me. The staffer who answered the phone growled that he'd send someone over. His tone told me it wasn't going to be a gentle removal so I waited beside Saul, who held the pen while he studied that day's Niche piece, a tiny golden statue of Ganesh, the Hindu elephant god.

— Saul, I just called your house. They said to come home right now.

No response.

— Someone's coming to get you, and they'll be here any minute. Wouldn't you rather go back on your own?

Still nothing. But he wasn't touching or disturbing anything, including the statue, so I decided to leave him where he was and tell Mom. Wu had found a clean pile of donated clothing and was lying in it, talking softly to himself, lost in a pretend world. She looked annoyed at the interruption and rolled the chair back from her desk.

— Saul's back, I said.

She reached across the piles of paper on the desk for the store phone. I waved her back.

— I called the home already. He's all right, I think. He isn't doing anything. I can watch him.

— Are you sure? I can come out.

— No, I think it'll be fine.

She paused, weighing things in her mind.

— All right. But let me know when someone from the home gets here.

Her tone told me that she wasn't yet convinced. Still, it was an effort to give me some independence and I felt a brief stab of sympathy, along with the urge to tell her Dad's secret. Why hadn't he told her yet? I felt like that guy who holds the rope before a tug-of-war begins. Knowing, as he feels the anticipatory energy of both teams making the rope hum in his hands, that if he waits too long, the whole thing will be lost: one of the teams always surges before it's supposed to.

A few minutes later, a van rushed up and parked in front of the store, scraping its rims against the curb. A dark-haired man slammed the driver's side door and strode in, making directly for Saul. He didn't even speak to me. Saul managed to shrug away the man's first grab for his arm and sat down on the floor, rocking back and forth, agitated. The man swore loudly and then threatened to break Saul's arm if he didn't move. Saul crouched even lower into himself, covering his head with his arms.

Filed under: Prick, Unimaginable.

My mother appeared, holding Wu, just as the skin on the man's neck grew red between the looping coils of the knots tattooed there.

— Stop that, she said.

— Lady, mind your own business.

— Anne, she said, folding her arms.

— What?

— That's my name, and this is my store, so it is my business.

The man stared at her, confused, choking out that we were the ones who had called, so if we wanted Saul out we should just stand aside and let him do his job. She stood fast with her arms folded as his anger rose. Saul, meanwhile, had begun to rock more violently. Wu began crying. The tension in that moment, in the midst of our anger and volume and confusion, was dense as iron.

— Jesus, look at him. Get out of the way, the man said.

— Calm down or I'll call the police.

— The police? Come on, I'm just—

New voices from the front of the store cut through it all.

— Saul! Are you okay?

Two blurs, one dressed in a red shirt and the other in blue, dashed in. Silence fell as Red and Blue, a couple of identical twins who spent their days wandering from dumpster to dumpster, knelt next to Saul, laid their hands on his shoulders and arms, and calmed him down. Saul brought his arms down and stopped rocking, and turned to face each girl as she spoke, smiling and nodding. Even Wu was transfixed, his sunken eyes bright as he witnessed the miracle.

— It's okay, Saul, we can go now, Blue said.

— Yeah. It's nice out, Red said.

The group home staffer looked at his watch. Mom and I looked down at the two girls as they ministered to Saul, absorbed by their selfless task, their bodies young yet their eyes faded and wise. They helped Saul to his feet, their thin limbs almost carrying him to the waiting van. Blue noticed me staring and smiled shyly. I hadn't realized I had followed them outside.

— We heard the yelling, she said.

— And Saul's a nice man, her sister chimed in.

They left holding hands. We had seen them around, of course, enough to know about a mother working nights on Barton Street and a father, homeless too, who refused to speak to them. Despite this, they remained polite, a heartbreaking paradox against a life that would harden them far too soon. Even as a clueless teenager my heart hurt when I saw them, but it was a conflicted, guilty pain. I wanted to hug away every bad thing but held back, too afraid to act.

After closing, we took the day's deposit across the park to the bank. Mom went ahead with the lock-bag while I hung back, moving slowly with Wu, who'd decided he wanted to walk on his own. I watched her, wondering how she would react to Dad's admission, assuming he ever told her. She had paused when we first stepped outside, and the evening sun's amber glow faded the dark smudges under her eyes. But it had been a momentary softening— her back and shoulders were tense as she moved, the grey canvas bag gripped too tightly under her arm. Wu toddled over to one of the trees, looked up, and started trying to climb its branchless trunk.

— That's not going to work, squirt.

— Tree!

He began pulling, his little arms barely getting around the small trunk, as though the obvious solution was to bring the tree down to the ground. His hands slipped and he thunked onto his butt. He frowned, looking at the dirty new abrasions on his palms and knees.

— Ow, he said. Rough.

As I helped him up, I bumped into his scraped knee, making him cry out from the sting. He gave me a sharp look, accusing, as though I'd somehow conspired to hurt him more.

— Sorry, Wu. Here, watch this.

I lifted his hands and blew on the scrapes, which were shallow, the skin barely broken. Trading germs for comfort.

— Better? I asked.

— No.

I waited. I knew this game.

— Yes, he said after a beat, drawing out the word like a long, sad note.

At the far end of the park, Mom looked around her as she crossed the street to the deposit slot. By the time she returned, Wu was again enthralled by the trees and their spindly trunks, babbling away about next time and climbing and that his knees would be all better. He insisted on holding both of our hands as we crossed King.

When we got home, Dad was in the kitchen, garrisoned in by a fort of white Chinese takeout containers.

— I ordered way too much, he said. I hope you're hungry.

— What are you doing home so early? Mom asked.

— I thought maybe we could talk tonight. About the store, and—

— Let's eat first, she said, sighing.

Leich arrived home just then, stomping up the stairs and dropping his backpack. He made a face for Wu but simply nodded at everyone else, throwing back up the wall of nonchalance he'd been working on since the robbery. As Mom went to the cupboard for plates, I grabbed Wu and plopped him into his booster seat. Dad leaned over and piled some crispy chow mein noodles on Wu's tray, which he rearranged into three neat little piles before cramming them in his mouth. And then we were all sitting at the table together, for the first time in a long, long time.

There was an awkward moment of silence before Mom laughed.

— It's like we forget how to do this, she said, reaching for the rice.

— It's nice, Dad said.

I wondered how quickly that could change, given what I knew about Dad. Leich studied his plate as he ate. Wu played with his piles of noodles. At some point we started talking, hesitant at first, like we were learning how to fit into each other's rhythms again. Dad caught my eye a couple of times. I looked away. It was awkward but comforting. There's that old expression, like ships in the night, and that's how our family felt at times, between Dad's long working hours, Leich's and my dashing around the city, Mom's store, her sick son with his disproportionate number of medical appointments, and so on. But we always came home. We crossed paths often enough to keep ourselves from forgetting each other's faces.

Would my dad lay it all out? The meal was a clever tactic, if that's what it was, relaxing everyone and putting us all in family mode before dropping his bomb. Amidst all the other bombs, of course: the robbery, losing the revenue from Luigi's and Razza's. Even if he hadn't lost his job, keeping the Weston would have been at least an uncertainty, at most a sentence of bankruptcy. How would Mom react? She'd been up and down and every stretch in between for the past while, so there was no way to know. The dream of running a business was concretely her own, as constant as sunrise and sunset, even after Dad left us and came back, even after the robbery. Before getting married, she'd drifted a lot, moving from temp job to temp job to support her activism in various cities. Dad always wanted to be a lawyer, even if he couldn't have envisioned ending up immersed in the corporate side of law. Owning the Weston kept his hippiness alive, and his job gave Mom a measure of financial security. Assuming he could keep his practice viable, that was.

Dad sat back and nodded at Leich and me.

— Could you take care of Wu for a while? Your mom and I need to have a talk.

— I'll take him. I could use some ice cream, Leich said. Want to come, Mutts?

— No, thanks.

I knew what was happening, but had been thinking of calling Peter, whom I hadn't seen since his fall at the fair.

— You should come, sis. It'll be fun.

— I'm all right—I'll just go to my room and shut the door.

— No. Really. It'll. Be. Fun.

Leich scooped Wu up and made for the door, stopping just before he got there to give me a meaningful look. He inclined his head towards King Street. I groaned and got up to follow my brothers.

— Why do I feel like this has been all planned out, Mom said, looking wearily at Dad, who got up to put on some tea.

On the sidewalk, I made my excuses and ignored Leich's half-hearted protests about bonding and quality family time—we both understood that he'd just wanted to get us out of the house. He hefted Wu onto his shoulders and walked west along King. I knew they'd walk to James Street and turn right, heading north towards Gino's, an Italian café that served Hamilton's best gelato and ice cream. Growing up, making that walk had been a ritual, a Sunday night pilgrimage for our family. I rode on Dad's strong shoulders like Wu was riding on Leich's—I wondered if Wu felt as secure as I had. I watched them go, waiting for Wu to look back, like he always did. Sure enough, thirty feet away he turned, waving and smiling the wrinkles from his face. I waved too.

As I pulled out my phone, I heard a yell from across the street. It was Peter, hobbling on two crutches towards the intersection. He moved slowly, the drivers stopped at the lights watching him the whole way as though his discomfort was the only interesting thing to see. Finally, he was in front of me, cheeks flushed, hunched over because the crutches were too low.

— What are you doing here?

— Your brother called, said your dad needed to talk with
    your mom.

Confirmation that Leich had known all along, and
hadn't become a willing accomplice just in the moment.
How much did he know?

— Did he say anything else?

— No, just that I should come over. I was having some
trouble with the cathedral anyhow, so—

— What's the problem?

— I'm fighting with some of the fine details.

— Columns, windows, benches—?

— Right, he said. They're called pews.

— Pews. Got it.

— I'm trying to be as accurate as possible. Art on the
    walls, statues in the chapels, that sort of thing. The
    statues are giving me grief. I can't seem to start
    any of them.

— Like writer's block, but the scale modelling version.

— All I have are all these tiny, empty spaces. Nooks.
    Chapels.

— Sounds depressing. How's the ankle?

He looked grateful for the change in subject.

— I'm already sick of the crutches, he said, his face bright-
    ening. Hey, maybe you could sell them in the store.

— I'm not sure who would—

I stopped myself. He had made a joke. We were friends
so we joked around, of course, but he was in pain, so right
then I couldn't have expected levity. I laughed—how
could I not?—and suggested we head over to the women's
monument at the end of the park, located on a prominent
square of concrete. Benches on four sides of the space
provided a view of the monument and the city beyond from

all four points of the compass. The bronze statue, velvety as chocolate, where Queen Victoria faced west with a male lion resting at her feet, was my favourite place to sit and watch the city bustle by—my favourite amongst many. I loved the spread of the old farmers' market, too, best taken in from a Relay Coffee barstool. The old train station in the north end stood sentinel, waiting for someone to make good use of the old facade, for the city to reclaim itself. And the emerging scene on James Street North, with its red brick facades, art galleries and studios, cafés and writers' nooks, and the revitalization efforts of its talented residents. But the statue in the park rose above them all, lion and queen, queen and lion, inverse to history's expectations.

Peter sat with a loud exhalation and raised his foot onto the bench. His eyes scanned the surrounding building facades, as though cataloguing what might have changed since seeing them last. With no room on the bench, I sat on the ground, crossing my legs and doing my best to avoid the black pennies of gum and smudged pools of spit on the cement. Peter noticed and frowned.

— Come up here. I can move my leg.

— Don't, I said. Keep it elevated.

— There's room—

— No, there isn't. I'm fine.

He opened his mouth to speak but closed it. Shook his head. I didn't go out of my way to sit on the gross things that ended up on the ground, of course, but there wasn't much I could do about it. In some ways, learning to take city grime in stride is an urban rite of passage for anyone who dares to love buildings and pavement. Peter had never been as comfortable with the city's filth as I was. He tended to look up, seeking out the higher features of the city.

He pointed at the monument.

— They cleaned her off, he said.

Sure enough, the white pigeon streaks were gone, leaving her crown and sceptre dark and clean. It was nice of him to notice, if a little odd. He knew I loved to come here but had never said anything about the monument before. I was touched. In that moment, I almost told him everything. Again.

He might not have heard me anyway. He'd closed his eyes and leaned awkwardly back onto the bench, his face drawn, as though his ankle had chosen right then to remind him of his discomfort. It didn't feel like the right time for saying much of anything, so I relaxed. It was busy in the park that evening, and the air was clean and clear. A strong westerly breeze had banished the exhaust from the steel mills to the east end of the city. Somehow the downtowners knew exactly when to be out, that certain days were best enjoyed outside. Peter and I were lucky to have gotten a bench at all.

After a while, he grew restless.

— It hurts to stand, but I can't sit for long either.

— What do you want to do?

— I should get home and lie down, maybe. But first—

He pulled out a little box from his pocket and handed it to me.

— What's this? What did you do—

— Just open it.

So I did. There were two parts, a metal base made of a slowly uncoiling serpent, and a glass egg that looked like someone had chopped off the top to get at the meat. The egg fit perfectly into the base, the two pieces light when apart but heavy together. The quality of the workmanship was excellent, the engravings crisp, the blown glass flawless.

My first thought was that it looked exactly like something we'd have found in the Niche, but that was impossible—I would have seen or known or heard about Peter finding his one thing. My second thought was how much it must have cost. I looked at him, questioning.

— It's a container for your desktop. An ink pot.

— Like for a fountain pen.

— Right. Old school.

— I don't know how to do calligraphy.

— It's more for posterity, you know?

— Hard to get nostalgic for dipping and blotting and getting ink everywhere.

— You don't have to use it. I just thought—

Peter's eyes had travelled to the ground, his mouth turned downwards at the corners. Shit, I thought. Nice one, Mutton. He's just given you a gift, and all you can do is focus on the practicality.

— Sorry, Peter. It's gorgeous.

— You think so?

— I do. When—where—did you find it?

He blushed.

— At the fair. When we were in the vendors' area and you went to the port-a-johns. I saw it earlier.

I'd give anything to be able to transport myself back to that moment to see my face. We had stuck together all day, from the falafel breakfast to his embarrassed dismissal of the security guards' offer to call an ambulance to when his aunt picked him up. My trip to the bathroom had taken a few minutes at most, so he must have been waiting for the chance to run back and get it. As he explained the meaning of the serpent and the egg and how it was a mark of pride for a writer to have a nice ink pot, it all started to come together.

My God, I remember thinking. He's crushing on me.

And I didn't have a response, aside from the brief misting of my eyes at just how thoughtful he had been in locating such a gift—could it have been more perfect? He was proud of himself for getting a good deal, too, and spent a good five minutes describing, in exuberant detail, how he had bargained the merchant down. In later years, I might have rolled my eyes about that—a girl doesn't want bargains, she wants the good stuff—but right then it blew past. It was an amazing gift. I still have it, and often think about how wonderful it would be to fill it, load an antique fountain pen with good ink, and write love letters to a cosmos that brought me such a good friend as Peter.

But right then I was more preoccupied by the knowledge that I didn't feel the same as he did.

He didn't say the words, though, which kept me from having to figure out how to respond. I also knew not to give the ink pot back, though it must have cost quite a bit, even after his valiant bargaining. Maybe it was enough to let the day end, clinging to the positive, rather than giving the wrong response. We got up and each slowly made our way home; by the time I darkened our door, the sky was purple and orange above the city, the buildings grey and strong against it.

There was a police cruiser parked in front of the store the next morning, sitting quietly, black and white and conspicuously clean. The cop inside had his head down, working on a laptop computer; the crackle of the radio and the soft clicking of keys drifted out through the open passenger window. Sounds seemed amplified that windless morning, especially in the lulls between waves of King Street traffic. As we closed the apartment gate the police officer, the small one who had taken our statements and hit on my mother, looked up and waved. He leaned towards the open passenger window and yelled out a greeting.

— Morning, kids! Is your mom available?

Mom had told us she wanted to disappear for a while into the spare room for a yoga session and Dad hadn't come out at all. Leich snorted softly—what seventeen-year-old enjoyed being called a kid?—reopened the door, and yelled up the stairs. She came down in her stretch pants, iPod in hand, like she hadn't had the chance to choose her yoga music. White earbuds dangled against her neon-green top, bouncing with each barefooted step like strange, postmodern jewelry. The officer stepped out and put on his hat as he moved around the cruiser towards her, smiling broadly and doing his best to keep his downward glances subtle.

I stared. Leich elbowed me in the ribs.

— Let's open up, he said. Mom'll tell us later.

We unlocked the front doors and fell into our opening routines. Ten minutes later, she came in, looked tiredly around, and asked if everything was ready for the day. Leich and I responded simultaneously in the affirmative; I had just sat on the stool behind the till and opened my novel, and he was getting ready to head back to the apartment.

— Essentially, there's no news, she said.

— They still haven't caught the guy, Leich said.

She shook her head, looked over to the patched bullet hole that Dad still hadn't sanded or painted, and sighed.

— Leich, I know you're leaving, but can you stay for a moment? I want to tell both of you what your dad and I talked about last night.

Leich and I listened. Dad had told her about his firm slashing through the ranks with an unexpected round of layoffs a couple of months before, how he'd hidden it from all of us as he lined up enough business to hang his own shingle, how hard it was to attract new interest in a tough market, and so on. In other words, she explained the very burden I'd borne for days, though the details of the layoff, the firm hiding behind insulting, generic terms like simple economics, was new information.

Leich took the news hard, exhaling loudly and leaning against the counter.

— God, that sucks, he said.

— He's doing his best, Mom said. He's optimistic.

— You don't sound very convinced, I said.

— No, I am. For all his faults, your father is—is—She paused a moment.

— Determined, Leich said.

Mom chuckled softly under her breath, her laugh lines deepening around her eyes.

— He is that, she said.

— We'll have to sell the Weston, Leich said.

I tried to act surprised but probably wasn't very successful.

— Your dad doesn't want to. He wants to keep the building even if it means going into the red for a while. I offered to close Second Chances, but—

— No way, Leich said. He knows how much the store means to you.

— We all do, Mom, I said. But still—

— I know, Mutton. I know.

Part of me admired Dad for trying to hold it together, but it just didn't make sense to keep the building. There's only so much blood a family can give. Simple economics indeed.

But then she relayed a new piece of the story. Before Dad was let go from the firm, The Outfit had made a visit to his office and told him to sell the Weston or face the consequences. There had been no witnesses, of course—the nasty little man knew the law—but the implied threat was obvious. No, Dad had told her, we have to do everything we can to keep him from getting the Weston.

— It's important for your father to fight him as long as we can, she said. For us to fight him together.

But her eyes weren't entirely convinced. She hadn't forgiven him for keeping the secret from her, a betrayal that had to have reopened former wounds. The words might have been easy to say—especially *fight* and *together*—but I knew that rebuilding trust would take longer. Then her eyes changed, becoming black as new pavement, and I knew her thoughts had shifted back to The Outfit.

— Because that man can't get his way again, she said. That—

Mom took a beat.

— That fucker, Leich said.

Mom and I drew a simultaneous breath—my brother didn't swear—but Leich just shrugged when he saw our expressions.

— Well he is, isn't he? Isn't that what were you going to say?

My mother smiled. Not the pursed, tight smile she occasionally allowed herself those days, but a beatific grin that made her look a dozen years younger.

— Something like that, she said.

Good job, Leich, I thought. Good job.

Mom leaned over and looked at the clock on the cash register, and her smile faded. She started to leave, saying something about watching Wu so Dad could start his day, whatever that looked like. At the door she paused and pulled out her iPod, put her earbuds in, and swiped through her music collection as though she was looking for just the right song to play. Her face reclaimed the seriousness Leich's outburst had chased away as she stared at the pedestrians, holding the bundled music player against her chest, awkward and silent. Then she walked out, leaving her two eldest kids to fill the store with a soundtrack of ideas, brainstorming ways to generate more interest in my mother's second-hand store.

It was a good day, a day focused on hope. Leich forgot that he had been about to leave and ran upstairs to grab his laptop, and we spent the rest of the morning using one of those free services to set up a website for the store. We argued good-naturedly about what pictures should be splashed across a new Facebook page and a handful of other social media sites. We added everyone we knew to our Twitter feed and scoured city hashtags for interesting—and hopefully well-connected—locals to follow. By lunchtime we had also come up with a strategy and loose schedule for promotion, where whoever was in the store would make a point of reaching out to at least one new person or business. It was a lot of fun; I couldn't remember the last time we'd spent so much time together, much less with a mutual interest.

Just as I was about to suggest—somewhat recklessly, you'll agree—we order in for lunch, Leich's phone chirped. He picked it up, read the text, and smiled briefly. Raising the phone to his ear, he mouthed a goodbye and walked out, leaving the computer glowing dully on the counter beside me. As he moved through the door, he nearly collided with a customer, offering a distracted apology before moving down the sidewalk and out of sight. She was pretty, maybe eighteen, and looked vaguely familiar.

— Your brother's cute, she said as she wandered deeper into the store.

What do you say to that? Thank you? You're right? I think so, too? Or maybe, in sister-snark, why do you care? More importantly, how nervy it was to say that to me, the sister. A girl could spend a lot of time reading too much into what others say, which I studiously tried to avoid, so I simply shrugged and went back to writing a script for the new site, highlighting the wonderful pre-chanced values to be had.

A few minutes later, I heard a squeal of delight from the back and I remembered who she was. That terrible laugh, like a dozen cheap mugs had been dropped on concrete, echoed through the halls at school, and Peter and I would sometimes make fun of it even though we didn't know her. Then she was at the till, breathless, eyes bright, holding a stained-glass sculpture of a blue-winged butterfly. She placed it on the counter as gently as her excited hands would allow. It was beautiful work, elegant and understated.

— You found the Niche item, I said, not thinking.

— I beg your pardon?

— How do you know my brother? I asked, trying to recover.

But there was no need. She simply smiled and dug her wallet from her oversized handbag, placing the exact amount I was thinking of asking for the butterfly in my hand.

— Oh, everyone knows Leich.

I took the money and rang it into the till. The girl—Renee, I remembered right then—took hold of the sculpture and walked out, staring at her purchase like it was the last item for sale on earth, before I could offer to wrap it up.

Everyone knows Leich. Really. What an interesting thing for her to say, and what an interesting thing for me to hear, given what I knew of my brother. And cute? That was a first, too, although maybe less surprising because sisters aren't supposed to think of their brothers as anything other than, well, brothers. Or are they? For a few minutes, I tried to see my brother like others might, but was distracted by the things I knew. His paperboy hat collection, his dark shirts and jeans, the bright chain he snapped onto his belt loops, his habit of twirling pens and other long objects around the base of his thumb, suspended against gravity. Or my jealousy of his driver's licence, the one he had gotten away from my parents' approval or knowledge, in defiance of their stance against owning a car. Another sort of gravity to defy.

Apart from the photo-clear image in my mind of his face on the day of the robbery, I kept circling around things *about* him, rather than things that *were* him. And I could only think about my fear. Again. And again. And how bad I felt that Leich would have a scar for life because of my inaction. The things I couldn't push away, I suppose, the things that *were* me, too.

A siren rushing along King snapped me from my thoughts. Its warbling was absent one second and pushing through the door the next, only to be cut off mid-wail as the vehicle, an ambulance, stopped in front of the store. Red lights bounced off the walls, whirling around, and I ran outside, not bothering to lock the store behind me. EMTs were trundling a gurney from the back of the vehicle. One had already opened the iron gate in front of our apartment door, and I ran up the stairs ahead of them.

My mother knelt on the floor in the living room, the cordless phone in one hand. My little brother lay unmoving on the hardwood, his eyes closed, wearing only a pair of Pull-Ups. I remember thinking how cold he must have been on the floor, how I had the urge to grab the afghan from the sofa and wrap him in it, tight enough to warm, tight enough to carry, tight enough to protect.

— What happened? I asked, dropping to my knees.

She didn't say anything. She just moved her hand up and down Wu's back and shook her head. I brought my head down to floor level and called his name. He opened his eyes. I could see him trying to move, trying to wave, but his entire left side wouldn't respond. Only half of his face smiled weakly, the other half remaining slack and unchanged.

Half a smile.

My heart—all of it, both sides, all four chambers—broke.

There were voices then, and firm hands pulling me to the side, urgent and steady. I let myself be half carried, feeling limp and unwilling to deal with any of it, into the waiting ambulance.

Much later, after the ambulance and waiting room and the doctors, Leich walked me home from the hospital. He waved away my father's offer to call a taxi for us, telling him it wasn't far, that a walk would do us both some good. Mom and Dad stayed behind, wanting to be there when the doctors decided on next steps. Leich and I had tried to stay, but they insisted, saying we should go home and at least attempt to rest. My mother and I had ridden to the hospital in the ambulance. The EMTs resisted, but relented when Mom told them we didn't own a car, packing Mom and me onto the bench opposite Wu. Mom told me later that I held Wu's hand so fiercely that an EMT had to pry us apart to get my baby brother out.

Wu had been knocked down by another stroke, his third. He was alive but unconscious, so no one seemed to know yet what the damage would be. The said the plan was to treat symptoms as they appeared and that they'd watch carefully to see if surgery was required. They stepped lightly around my little brother's condition; no one knew much about how progeria would affect his recovery from the stroke.

It was good for Leich to walk me home. We needed the space. Three strokes. For a three-year-old. The rest of us picking up pieces after they fell. Shouldn't families be able to keep them from falling in the first place?

We didn't talk much on the short walk back to King and Hughson. When we arrived, the Satan's Falafel cart was in front of our store, with Mr. Ahmad sitting on his stool in front of the shop door. He said that as soon as he saw the ambulance pull away, he closed up his cart, wheeled it over to guard our property, knowing that we had probably forgotten to lock up. He stood when he saw us, placed his hands on our shoulders, and asked if we were hungry. That was it. He didn't pry for details, he just met us where we were in that moment, knowing we would share when we were ready. And I was hungry, much to my amazement. Really hungry, in fact. Leich, too.

After, our bellies full, we bade Mr. Ahmad good night and closed up the shop. While Leich brought the cash drawer to the safe in the back, I tidied the cash register area of our social networking notes and ideas. My laptop, still open, had gone into hibernation mode. When I woke it up, our Facebook page was still open in the browser. A little red circle and a tiny number one peeked out from the top of the page. I clicked on it. The first item in the Second Chances timeline was a wall posting by someone whose name I didn't recognize.

— *Ur store luks amazing.*

I sat back, happy despite the stress of the day. Leich laughed out loud when he saw it even though his eyes were as red and heavy as my own. That breathless excitement was exactly what we had hoped to achieve.

The last few days of July had been hot and humid. The air, heavy and moist, had kept the pollution low to the ground, a perpetual haze surrounding the buildings like a dirty veil. Every day the weather forecasters had, without success, predicted thunderstorms to break the humidity, so no one trusted them anymore. The store's old AC unit had gone down on the ninth day of the heat wave with a pathetic clunk, comical in its finality. We set up dusty fans from storage, which succeeded more in stirring up mustiness than cooling the air. Second Chances had always smelled like a thrift store, but we had long been immune; now even we noticed it.

We forced ourselves to leave the door open all day.

On those kinds of days, people moved as little as possible. The city turned on the fountain in the park across the street and the homeless jostled with the army of shelter folk for valuable space in the mist. The upside was a boom in business for Satan's Falafel. Mr. Ahmad barely kept up with demand. There were no trees at his end of the park, so he combatted the sun by standing in a shallow pail of water for a few minutes at a time, dropping in an occasional ice cube from the drink cooler to keep the temperature down. Leich and I called it Satan's AC.

It was the first Tuesday of the month again, Guild night, so I tried to write something about the heat—I certainly hadn't been doing much work on my story—as I sat in front of the store on an old wicker chair, sweating enough for two people. With its southern exposure, the storefront only enjoyed a bit of shade from the spindly ginkgo trees sprouting from the sidewalk planters. You knew it was hot when being in the half-sun on a city sidewalk was preferable to the full shade indoors. I wasn't having much success with writing—even my hands were sweating.

A low whirring sound announced the arrival of Mrs. Nyman, an elderly lady whose daily activities seemed to consist of driving her Rascal—one of those battery-operated medical scooters—around, stopping here and there to sit and read one of the romance novels she took out from the Central Library. She backed up, the Rascal beeping like a dump truck, into a patch of shade before pulling out her book. I found her fascinating, both as a member of the downtown core's cast of characters, but also for her sad smile. She always gave me a wave but never said anything beyond hello. I'd been hesitant to introduce myself—a strange thing, as I wasn't usually afflicted by shyness—and only learned her name when the head priest at St. Paul's dropped by Second Chances one day and asked about her. Right now she might have had the best patch of shade in all of downtown and looked quite comfortable as she paged through a dusty pink paperback with a man and a woman on the cover competing over who had the nicest chest.

— Have to use a pencil on a day like today, she said.

I looked up, not quite believing she had spoken.

— For your writing. It won't smudge like that fancy gel pen you're using.

Having closed the romance novel, she watched me with a bright mix of curiosity and satisfaction, although I could tell that the sadness she always carried wasn't completely gone.

— That's okay, I said. The writing is probably better smudged so no one can read it.

She gave me a look.

— You're fishing.

— Fishing?

— For a compliment.

— No, it's just that—

— Not very pretty, especially sweaty and bothered as you are.

I looked down at my page, blurry and sodden, and at the edge of my hands, grey with wet ink. She wasn't wrong. I closed my notebook. I'd thought that churning out a short piece of flash fiction or even a poem would feel good, not just to keep my mind from the heat, but also to regain a bit of normalcy. Wu was recovering as well as anyone could have expected, his lethargy fading. But the rareness of his condition left far more questions than answers, no matter how many smiles he gave or how hard he tried to make the limbs on his left side work like normal. More questions. The police hadn't closed the case on the robbery but they weren't spending too much time on it either. Leich's wound had healed well, but the scar tissue often looked pink and angry, accusatory almost, especially in the heat. If Mom and Dad had made a decision about the store or the Weston, they weren't telling us. I was doing my best to act like my regular self around Peter, hoping we could just carry on like before.

— Besides, I hear you're very good, Mrs. Nyman said.

From whom, I wanted to know, but I gave her a thanks and a smile instead.

— I have a story for you, if you're interested.

You'd think I would have been jumping all over myself to hear it, but truthfully I wasn't sure I wanted to. Living downtown supplied my creative mind with reams of great material, but also hardened my social side. Too many sad stories, maybe, with too few good ones to balance the load. Yet Mrs. Nyman had fascinated me from the first time I saw her reading her trashy novels in front of the store, and my curiosity made the decision for me.

— I'd love to hear your story.

— Now, did I say it was *my* story?

I closed my mouth and waited for her to speak. And she did, telling me about a priest and a bunch of kind nuns from the old Catholic parish on Victoria Avenue who decided to do something good for their city. This was a long time ago, when social programs for the poor were typically run out of church basements, she said, seldom used by out-of-work mill workers who often cast their blame on God. So the priest and the nuns decided to set up a soup kitchen in an abandoned storefront in the Weston Arcade—our storefront. The neighbourhood was even rougher then, sooty and forgotten, as though the money from the prosperous mills left the city almost as soon as it was made. There was a lot of prostitution and drug abuse, and abandoned babies began appearing in front of the glass doors in the mornings, the perceived judgment lessened by the irreligious nature of a storefront. When she used the word judgment, her eyes misted over and her voiced hitched.

It's not hard to figure out, right? She, too, walked away from a baby, leaving him on the same stretch of concrete sidewalk where we sat. She didn't say another word, but I still saw what happened. It was still dark when she stumbled to the Weston and laid her newborn boy in front of the locked soup kitchen doors. She was sweating from the warmth of the stuffy overnight heat and the shame of her actions. Tears streamed down her face as she walked away from the child. The city was in the throes of a heat wave then, too. I couldn't believe how clearly I saw everything, like it had been recorded just for me in perfect HD.

— You see it too, she said.

I nodded.

— That's why I come here. I still see it, but only from this sidewalk.

— I wonder how that's possible.

— Can't say for sure, but there it is.

With that, Mrs. Nyman wiped her eyes, threw the novel into the basket at the front of her Rascal, and retracted her umbrella. She gave a little wave—there seemed now to be so much more experience in the many wrinkles on her hands—and whirred away, leaving me and my sweaty self alone in front of Second Chances, wondering about magic and the power of place. About the history hiding right in front of us. Family. A city's paths and structures. Faith and about people doing good things for each other.

About everything most important, maybe.

Eventually, I gave up trying to write, the heat simply sucking anything original or interesting out of me before I could sweat it onto the page. I grabbed my laptop and tried responding to a few of the tweets and postings to the store's Facebook page, but the heat of the computer on my lap was sickening. So I just sat there with a paper fan I found on one of the store's shelves, the faded cranes and Chinese characters pushing warm air at my face, blurred but ineffective. We had a few customers, but as soon as they encountered the stifling air inside, they left as quickly as they came. It was a long, slow day.

A few city workers, shirtless under their orange safety vests, came by early in the afternoon. They parked their dented and dirty truck and proceeded to unload a host of unfamiliar things, traffic cones and tripods and instruments and scuffed plastic cases, swearing so much the humid air turned blue around them. When they were done, they sat on the tailgate and waited for someone to tell them what to do. After a while, The Shirt, our ward councilman, drove up, his car looking as if it had been washed and shined just moments before. He pulled a hard hat, clipboard, and tubes of rolled-up plans from his trunk and an engineer in a white hard hat tumbled from the passenger seat. Together, they yelled at the city workers, who grumbled and began to set up their gear.

I called Mom to tell her what was going on.

— He's probably just taking measurements for his precious casino, she said.

— I thought the shopkeepers had fought it.

— They did, but it isn't dead. There's too much money working the back rooms of city hall.

The small businesses in the ward knew about and opposed The Shirt's latest revenue generator, a proposed hotel and casino complex. He saw the quick dollars the complex would generate while the rest of us protested how it would in reality draw precious food and entertainment revenues away from small businesses in the core. We opposed the exploitation, too, of people who'd lose more than they could afford. The councilman probably wouldn't get his way, but still put on a performance of promoting the idea and, on the hottest day of the year, donning his hard hat like groundbreaking was just around the corner. He wanted our block as much as The Outfit did, but unlike his less legally concerned competition was encumbered by bureaucracy. Another worry.

— Hey, Mom, how are you doing?

— I'm getting there.

— Can I—

— Let me know if anything else happens, all right?

Cut me off again. Too much of that going on lately.

— But—

— You'll be fine. Talk to you later.

— Okay, I said.

We hung up. Interesting. She reassured me that I'd be fine even though I'd called her to keep her informed. A distracted reversal she probably wasn't even aware of.

I resumed my vigil. For half an hour the councilman and his cronies measured and surveyed and swore before packing themselves back into their superheated vehicles and disappearing into the haze. I closed my eyes and tried to imagine something, anything, to write.

— Are you open?

A middle-aged couple stood in front of the store, holding hands.

— We are, but the AC is down so it's hot in there, I said.

— That's fine, they replied in unison before heading into the store.

I stayed outside. A few minutes later, his T-shirt darkened by sweat, the man came out and told me they would like to pay. We went back in together. His wife stood next to the till, fanning herself with one of the city tourist brochures Mom couldn't say no to. But they looked thrilled at having found the day's Niche item, a silver brooch with an animal—a dog, I thought—chasing its tail. I offered to polish it for them, but the woman shook her head.

— No, we'll do that before the wedding.

— It's our Something Old, the man declared.

— For our daughter, she said.

They looked like such a nice couple, I thought, complementing each other's rhythms, still in love, excited about being able to participate in their daughter's wedding preparations. We went through the process, them asking the price, me responding with an amount far, far lower than they had anticipated, them happily offering more, me refusing, them paying and thanking me profusely. I always enjoyed that part, an affirmation that maybe I was doing something right.

— She knew we'd find something here, the woman said.

I asked her how they'd heard about Second Chances.

— Oh, Beth found it on Facebook.

— Or maybe Tweeter, he said.

I smiled at that.

— But we'd had a feeling we needed to come down here anyhow, she said. Talked about it for a few days.

— Then Beth called, he said.

— And the decision was made for us. Do you have a business card?

I handed her a dusty old card with the store's information. She asked for a couple more, saying she would give them to her friends. As I handed the cards over and thanked them for their business, I felt like calling Leich right then and there to tell him that at least some of our online efforts had worked.

The couple walked out like they had come in, hand in hand.

Only three of us showed up for Guild night at Duster's, which had working AC and was blissfully cool. The heat had brought a few others in, too, unusual for a Tuesday, and Jenny bustled around the bar, busy as a squirrel. The others had sent their apologies; Marvin didn't feel like leaving his place, and Sara was in the hospital for some routine procedure she wouldn't divulge. The three of us sat where we always did, but without the other tables pulled in it seemed like we just didn't occupy enough space.

I endured the customary good-natured ribbing about showing up for a second meeting without anything to critique. Sara had emailed Eleanor her latest poem, asking to be workshopped in absentia; after passing out copies and spending a few silent minutes reading, Bart threw his hands up in the air and said he was lost. Eleanor and I burst out laughing, having been thinking the same thing.

Bart's latest—how he managed to be so prolific when he spent so much of his non-work time hitting the bottle was beyond me—bore a startling similarity to almost every other story he submitted, and I was pretty sure Eleanor and I were having the same struggle: how to tell him to try something new without setting him off.

— But the zombie blood is dark blue this time, he said. Like ink. And they're taller than the humans.
— Maybe the zombies could come from somewhere other than a convent in your next one, I said.
— No way. Nowhere else could work so good.

I caught Eleanor's eye and she nodded. We knew this routine well: we'd workshop Bart's stories until it became obvious nothing more could—or would—be done, and then we'd make eye contact, our pre-arranged two-minute warning. It happened every meeting. Thankfully he never caught on, allowing us to transition more easily into the next piece.

Which that night happened to be Eleanor's. It was tradition that she'd read her story aloud to us; we'd sit back, close our eyes, and drink in her words. She had written a charming story about a small paleolithic family living in caves, where the patriarch decides one day that the whole family will make ochre hand outlines on the cave walls. She wrote the entire story without dialogue, which was a huge challenge, yet created a multilayered story that was at once funny and extraordinarily sad, especially the climax, which involved the family solving the problem of the youngest child, a toddler, having no idea how to blow paint from his mouth.

There was nothing to critique—we both loved it, absolutely and completely. Bart smiled at the end, coughing behind the glass as he drained his third beer to cover his emotions. Eleanor was an exceptional writer, one of those rare souls who could have won prize after prize if she had wanted to, but only wrote for our tiny writer's group. She would change her mind later that year, telling me that the summer's events had helped her realize that others might benefit from her stories. Urban legend in the writing world has her marching into a publishing house in Toronto, grabbing an editor by the ear, and becoming one of the world's most well-loved authors overnight.

There was a sniffling sound beside me. At some point during the reading, Jenny had come by to take our orders and became ensnared by the story. Her features had softened; she wiped a tear away with a rough, thick finger.

— That was good, Eleanor, she said. Uh, really good.

She coughed to cover a slight hitch in her voice and lifted her chin at Bart.

— Got a double order of fries and suicide wings.

He looked up, already a little drunk, ready to argue.

— You're still on the clock, she said. Remember?

— Sure, boss. Got it.

Jenny grunted and turned back towards the bar. Bart tied on his apron and eased himself up from his seat, leaving Eleanor and me alone at the table. There was nothing left to read and it was still early, so we sat and talked. I told her about Mrs. Nyman's story and asked if she had ever heard about the soup kitchen and the abandoned children.

— Sure, I remember, said Eleanor. That kind of thing doesn't get forgotten.

— Can you tell me anything else?

She took a sip of her now-warm beer and set the glass down on a stained paper coaster.

— I was just a little girl, but I remember the ruckus it caused. People were upset.

— Why? It was a charity—

— Sure, but in those days that kind of thing was out of sight, out of mind. People hated that the priests set up right there on King, plain for everyone to see.

— Did it go on for long?

— No, but lots of kids were left there. Not all of them survived either.

— That's sad.

— True, but hopeful, too, even if it's an incomplete kind.

— Would it be wrong to say that it's a great story?

— Not at all. You should write it.

— Why me?

— You're part of that history—your building, your store.

— I'm not sure I could do it justice, I said.

She made a dismissive sound.

— There's no one better suited. The power of that place might be in its stories—who better to get them onto the page than a writer who lives and works right there?

— I'd worry about getting it right.

— You will—some stories won't let themselves get told wrong, if that makes any sense.

In my peripheral vision, I saw someone walk up to the bar. Black jeans and shirt. Chucks. Shoulder bag. Black and pink striped scarf. Jenny threw the bar towel over her shoulder, shelved the pint glass she'd been drying, and hooked a thumb over her shoulder towards us. The guy walked to the back and stood beside the table.

— Hi. I'm—

He didn't finish. He saw me and gave a nod, his chin lifting ever so slightly. Then he waited, like I was supposed to fill the gap he'd left, like it was up to me to make sure he was acknowledged. I didn't. After a moment, Eleanor started to fidget, her eyes moving between the guy—The Scarf, I thought, that's this idiot's name—and me and back again.

— You were at the fair, he finally said. Behind the trailers.

— I was, I said. And you were smoking.

I said smoking like I could taste the tar.

— Technically, I wasn't. I tried to bum one off you and your boyfriend, remember?

— Peter? He's not my boyfriend. He's—

Wait, I thought. Stop. Why do I need to explain Peter to this stranger? But then The Scarf grinned at me, a genuine smile, as though what I'd just said was the best news he'd ever heard. Good, I imagined him saying. That means you're free. Which was pathetic, and yet against every instinct I felt my own mouth creeping into a smile. My heart rate increased. There was warmth, too, somewhere and everywhere. And then it didn't seem like such a bad idea to explain about Peter and me. In fact, what a convenient way to signal that—

Eleanor leapt to her feet, interrupting my reverie and saving me from a gushing, runaway oblivion, and pulled out the chair Bart had been sitting on. The Scarf unslung his bag and put it on the table in front of him as he sat. I studied my iced tea with a sudden need to ponder the paper composition of the sodden coaster and the beaded condensation on the side of the glass. Eleanor asked if he'd come for the writer's group.

— I was wondering if you're accepting new members, he said. I write some things. I mean, I like to write.

— Well, of course you can join, Eleanor said. We're always looking for talent. Right, Mutton?

— I, um, yes.

As Eleanor introduced herself, I crawled back into myself. Not my proudest moment. He gave his name, but it sped past—I was too focused on worrying about how my name must have sounded to him. I was also annoyed at how quickly Eleanor had agreed to let him in, even though she'd extended the same grace to me. The Guild wasn't a closed group or anything, but it wasn't a social club: we were friends who helped each other write better. We'd had people sit in, but they faded away after a session or two—enjoying the group's intense process took a certain personality. No wonder we were so close—we had the convenient, central location and a mutual love of the pen, but it took real effort to balance the work and the play. Peter was my best friend and the Guild was the completion of my small outer friendship circle. After a few moments, I realized that Eleanor and The Scarf had gone quiet and were watching me.

— I'm sorry?

— He was just saying he would love to bring something next month.

— If that's all right, he said, looking at me.

As though it was my decision. Like the fifteen-year-old junior member was the gatekeeper with the final say on whether he could join. This teenage boy. Me, the teenage girl. Eleanor beamed at the two of us from her side of the table like an overbearing aunt who'd just discovered a propensity for matchmaking. I wanted to glare at her but couldn't—the blushing had started, an unstoppable creep of embarrassment and, worse still, excitement.

— Of course it is, I said. The Scarf joining, I mean. You. Can join. If you want.

— Great, he said.

— It's settled, then, Eleanor said.

He turned to me with great solemnity.

— The Scarf will, of course, bring enough copies for everyone.

He looked up at me and Eleanor and smiled. I smiled back. Of course I did. Apparently there are times when your face muscles are merely extensions of your muddled hormones. If the earth had stopped rotating in that instant I would have been launched into the vacuum of space with that same loopy grin, thinking that maybe he didn't look so bad in black and did they make Chucks in my size and if that scarf looped onto that bag's strap wasn't the sickest thing ever then I was just a lost cause, like, right?

Yes, I was that far gone.

Eleanor, satisfied, made her excuses, gathered up her binders and pens, and vanished, leaving The Scarf and me alone at the table. Jenny gave a little nod from the bar, a knowing nod, before studiously ignoring the two underage patrons holding court in the rear. The conspiracy widening, as it were. So, what next? Oh, nothing juicy, just a lot of nervous small talk and explorations of shared interests—we had a lot of those, which was terribly exciting—and the hint of a second meeting. I'd never had a boyfriend, and hadn't worried about it too much, but it was easy to slip into the *possibility* of having one in my near future.

Fate, Unavoidable.

When I called home and asked to stay at Duster's a little longer, my mother said it was fine but to be quiet when I came in. It had taken her a long time to get Wu to sleep, probably because of the humidity, and she sounded exhausted. In the end I didn't make a sound when I walked up our stairs, distracted by the new digits in my phone. As I padded between bedroom and bathroom, I kept turning my phone on to look at his contact photo, which I'd snapped at Duster's, the bright little glow moving with me through the darkness like a hopeful, dancing firefly.

I woke up late, grabbed my phone, threw on some jeans, and headed into the kitchen. Everyone was already there. No one looked at me as I poured some orange juice into one of Wu's plastic cups and stood next to the table.

Mom and Dad liked to say that they "retired" as hippies soon after they met at an anti-war rally. They fell in love and suddenly the idea of family and responsibility and a settled existence appealed to them more than the shiftless, nomadic lifestyle they enjoyed as singles. They still wore old protest shirts and Birkenstocks around the house and on weekends, and tried to keep up with the latest sustainable practices, but their rabidity for issues had been knocked into remission by a pragmatic approach to life. Dad dabbled in real estate and wore bespoke suits, and Mom had a particular love of electronic gadgets and synthetic yoga wear. The neighbourhood still saw them as the local green nuts, though. I wondered what all of that would look like in the future, given the changes we were living through.

Wu noticed me.

— Yay, Mutton!

I smiled at my baby brother and gave him a quick kiss on the top of his head. He squirmed, pleased but awkward, and knocked some of his Cheerios onto the floor. His left side hadn't fully returned to normal, so his greetings were still lopsided. The doctors had been impressed by how well he seemed to be rallying from the stroke, but stopped short of using words like full recovery.

— Did you have a good sleep, buddy?

— Yes, Wu said.

He said it as though the question deserved only the most studied consideration, before reaching for Mom's iPad and swiping at the news article she was reading. The text on the page, smeared with milk, scrolled down.

— He did, actually, Mom said. Slept right until breakfast.

— That's great, I said.

— Yep, she said. Right, Wu? But how about next time you go down easy, too?

Wu giggled and she went back to her news, trying to find the lines she'd lost.

My phone beeped in my pocket, drawing a raised eyebrow from Leich, which I did my best to ignore. I turned away from his prying eyes and switched it to silent mode.

— *r u busy today*

— *no. Meet?*

— *cntrl libry? 10?*

I thought, Yes, yes, a thousand times yes! I might not have actually had that thought, but when I remember how receiving that text felt, those are the words that pop into my much older brain.

— *ok*, I wrote.

Mom straightened up, shut down the iPad, and started wiping the cereal gunk from Wu's face. She was running the store that day, and I was on the schedule to help her open. Wu was coming down, too—even though he'd been feeling better, Mom preferred to keep him close by. Leich agreed to come in if Wu needed a different environment, or if trying to corral his diminished but still substantial energy proved too much for Mom. After opening, I was free for the day, which meant I would be able to head over to the library without anyone noticing. Mom unstrapped Wu from his booster and let him down to the floor to run around. She looked at my jeans and sleep-stuffy T-shirt with a raised eyebrow.

— Do you want some breakfast before we open?
— No, thanks. Not hungry.
— You can't run on an empty tank, kiddo.
— The fridge is twenty feet from the store, Mom, I said, rolling my eyes. I won't starve.

She looked surprised at my reaction, but said nothing before disappearing down the hall to change out of her yoga gear.

She came out a few minutes later in her standard summer uniform of Birkenstocks, cut-off jean shorts, and an embroidered linen shift. I helped Wu walk down the steps—how big they were for such little legs—as Mom held the door and the gate open. It was already quite warm when we got down to the sidewalk, the air still and close, stirred slightly by the traffic. Another scorcher.

There were two people in front of the shop doors, an older woman with blue hair and an aluminum cane, and a guy wearing a well-worn safety shirt and muddy boots. Mom looked at him, puzzled, then brightened.

— Oh good, you're here for the AC, she said.
He scratched his head.
— Sorry, no, he said. Just some shopping.
— Me too, said the old lady. Been waiting for twenty minutes.
— We don't open for another few minutes, I said.
— That's all right—I don't mind waiting, she said. I couldn't sit still this morning anyhow.

— Me too, the man said. Fidgeted all through breakfast, drove the wife crazy—she practically kicked me out the door. Funny, eh?

This was a first—we'd never had people waiting for us when we arrived. Mom dug in her pocket for the keys, opened the door, and asked them to wait while we turned on the lights and got things ready. I could tell that she wanted to talk about it, but my mind was on my library meeting a couple of hours later. Making plans without anything to plan for. While Mom went to the safe, I grabbed an old stuffed animal, a baby panda missing one of its button eyes, and gave it to Wu to play with behind the counter. Mom put the Niche item onto a rear shelf—carelessly again, I noted—too quickly for me to determine what it was, and brought the cash drawer forward.

I looked around the shop to make sure everything was in its place before letting the customers in. They moved with the remarkable purpose of bargain hunters, scanning the shelves and racks with identical efficiency, even though they had arrived separately. Neither found anything to purchase—not even the Niche item, whatever it was—and departed the store within a few minutes. The old lady even failed to notice Wu, which was unheard of—old people always, always noticed him, and always, always avoided asking what was wrong with him.

— What a strange pair, Mom said.

— Yeah, I said, before heading out myself, thinking about what my library meeting at ten o'clock might bring.

I arrived early and had to endure inquiring looks from the information desk on the sprawling first floor of the library. There was a line forming by the open-access computers, eager and anxious faces waiting for the next available machine to tackle Facebook and job hunting and impervious government forms. The library had been designated by the city as a safe cool spot, where anyone could escape the heat. I shivered against the cold. The library must have been running its AC at full blast for the entire heat wave, long enough for the cold to penetrate the concrete floors and pillars.

Everything changes. A couple of years before, the entire building had been renovated, reborn from floor after floor of musty shelves and yellowing paper as a leaner social and communication space. While I had enjoyed seeing old books, I loved the new breathing space and the bright natural light that seemed to penetrate almost everywhere. The library had long been a favourite place, and I spent hours and hours there reading and writing—people-watching, too, with a halfway house and Sally Ann shelter across the street supplying lots of inspiration for my characters. There weren't many places in a teeming, needy downtown where an introverted fifteen-year-old could feel comfortable, but the library was one of them.

I wondered if The Scarf felt the same way, or whether he was tailoring our outing to my preferences. On that day, the unknown was unsettling—the librarians on the top floor might have felt the nervous vibrations from the girl fidgeting on the first.

He came in through the mall entrance, saw me, and smiled.

— Hi, he said.

— Hi.

An illustrious start, to be sure, after which we just stood there smiling instead of talking.

— I love this place, he finally said.

— Me too. I come here. A lot. I think it's the windows.

My words came out in a rush—I'd been holding my breath. He nodded towards the stairs and said he wanted to show me something. We walked up to the third floor. At the top, he stopped, turned to me, and apologized.

— I never asked if you were hungry. Wanted to eat.

Outside. Before doing library stuff.

— I'm fine, thanks.

— Or, uh, thirsty. Are you?

I shook my head, reassured at the slight tremor in his voice—his relief was as obvious as mine. He seemed to regain equilibrium and led me to the back corner of the floor, where a few cubicles sat in the shadows of the non-fiction stacks, and pointed to one of the cubicles.

— That's my writing spot.

Which explained why I hadn't seen him before. Yes, lots of people streamed through the library every day, but after a while many of the faces are familiar. Hamilton never hid itself.

— I like the fourth floor, I said. More light and space.

I normally wandered the fourth floor, which the library had left open for reading and studying, like a nomad, trying never to take the same chair two days in a row. He preferred routine, the sameness of the third floor stacks, the quiet. His cubicle was unremarkable, the veneer worn through where arms and elbows rubbed. But it was clean, unlike its neighbours that boasted innumerable graffiti tags and pencil doodles, and I felt disappointed at that, as though he should have carved our initials there with a desperate, love-chewed fingernail. I shook my head, banishing that thought right away—if you give infant, irrational ideas the space to grow, they become stubborn and uncontrollable teenagers.

— One more thing, he said.

He led me to the area beside the elevators, where local historical documents, photos, and the like were stored. The librarian—who looked the part, right down to the horn-rimmed glasses and worn cardigan—gave the slightest of nods when he waved to her. He led me into a musty room filled with leather-bound volumes and mouldy paper boxes, walked right through and stopped in front of a door at the back. A security lock blinked its red light at us from the wall beside the door. He looked over his shoulder, checking to see if we were alone, then gave a quick turn of the knob and a simultaneous pull so the door thunked against the frame. The lock released with a sharp sound, the door opened with a sharp hiss, and we were inside. He turned towards me and smiled.

— Security lock's been broken for months.
— Are you sure we should—what if—
— We'll be fine. They don't know.

It was even colder in that little room, and it smelled of brittle and dry paper rather than the mildew and old ink you'd expect, like the books had skipped those stages. There were no traditional shelves, either, just big grey slabs of metal lined up against one side of the room. He stepped to the third or fourth slab and pushed a button. With a dull rumble, the slabs separated one at a time, creating narrow passages as they moved along thin, recessed tracks on the floor. When a space appeared next to where he stood, The Scarf released the button and gave me a mischievous look.

— Like magic, right?

He disappeared into the space—I followed, of course—and took from a shelf a large volume with oxidized clasps and cracked leather. It opened slowly, yawning almost, like it had to breathe itself back into the present. He handed it gently over to me. Inside, the yellowed pages were covered by beautiful, handmade calligraphy. Most of the letters were familiar, but it could have been written in Sanskrit for how little I understood.

— This is the oldest item in the library, he said.

— How did you find it?

— I heard a librarian talking about it while she was giving someone a tour. I snuck in after.

I was no expert in ancient texts, but it was a religious book of some sort, judging by the detailed illustrations. Every halo, heavenward gaze, and reverent pose was painted by hand, the style reminiscent of church paintings from the Middle Ages I'd seen in art class.

— How old is it?

— If I heard the library lady right, it's more than eight hundred years old, The Scarf said.

— Why would they keep it here and not in a museum?

— Maybe it was donated or something.

— It's beautiful.

And it was. I haven't been back to check, but the likelihood that the secure, climate-controlled room tucked away on the third floor of the Central Library has never had the locks checked and changed has to be small. Still, holding such history in your hands, the quality of the work, isn't something you forget—the old book exuded loveliness through the skin, almost. Absorbed as I was—maybe the Niche and all the second-hand items in the store had made me more appreciative of such things—I lost track of time until he leaned over all that beauty and kissed me. Then I nearly dropped it.

Was it a long kiss? Who knows. At the end he sat back and looked at me with large, expectant eyes. He'd tasted like he'd chewed gum for too long.

— Shit, I said.

Right at the instant The Scarf had pressed his awkward lips against mine, I'd thought of Peter sitting on that bench and giving me that ink pot. Imagining how he'd feel if he knew. Shit indeed.

Not what The Scarf was expecting. He stumbled over platitudes, trying to reclaim some dignity, and reshelved the book. In the end, I had to block the gap and keep him between the shelves to work through my own damage control—he wasn't the only mortified one—to the point where he actually laughed. There are some forms of awkwardness you have to laugh at—the trick is to come out the other side resolving to laugh the next time, too.

The horn-rimmed librarian didn't look up when we came out a short time later, but it must have been painfully apparent we weren't only doing research in the local history archives. My head was spinning for so many reasons. Yes, it was my first kiss, undertaken with the finest discomfort first kisses can offer. Yes, I was excited about what might happen next. Yes, I was worried about Peter finding out. But you know what? The memory of that incredible book was heady; what it had witnessed in its centuries-long journey to that shelf, the stories it could tell. If you don't believe in magic, you should hold something like that in your hands. You will.

I saw them at about the instant I realized The Scarf and I were holding hands. Two large men in dark suits—nice suits—stood like obelisks at the entrance to the archives section, watching everything from behind dark glasses. Their boss, The Outfit, was poring over charts on one of the large tables. I pulled on The Scarf's hand, hoping to leave without being seen, and headed towards the elevators.

— Mutton, is it?

The obelisks moved just enough to let me know that leaving wasn't an option. We turned. The Outfit looked over his reading glasses and motioned us over. It was not a request, of course.

— I do not believe I have had the pleasure of meeting
   your friend.

He was wearing gloves, of all things, thin brown driving gloves. He picked them off one finger at a time and extended a hand to The Scarf. They shook, my date as nervous as a lamb tied to a stake. Probably thinking about why anyone would wear gloves in a heat wave. Someone who didn't want to leave a mark, I thought.

The Outfit turned to me.

— How are you? How is your mother?

I gave a bland reply, not wanting to engage with him. I glanced at the table and saw that the top chart was of an intersection a few blocks west of our own. He saw me, smirked, and leafed through the charts underneath. Pulling out one near the bottom of the pile, he laid it flat in front of us. It was a schematic of the intersection of King and Hughson, with the various streets and buildings marked in bold indigo.

— Anyone can come here and ask for these—the city
   makes it so easy to keep an eye on things.

— That's our corner, I said.

— Of course! I have not forgotten the Weston Arcade,
   my dear. I cannot stop thinking about it, actually. It
   has become one of my favourite places.

My poor date. He just stood there, looking confused and nervous, as I waited for The Outfit to let us go. He brought his hands up, adjusting the perfect Windsor knot at his throat, the tie's shade of blue a perfect match for the lines on the charts.

— You come here often, yes?

It was cool in the library, but his question made me imagine a single bead of sweat journeying from my shoulder blades to my lower back.

— Yes.

— I do also. I could have these brought to my office, but it is so important to go where people are. So they do not forget me.

He looked me in the eye so hard it stung, forcing me to glance away, before leaning back over his charts. I tasted metal. Copper, maybe. He made a dismissive motion with his manicured hand. The goons stepped back. You are now permitted to leave, the motion said.

We left the library and walked into Jackson Square in a daze, attempting to carry on with our date. We shared a plate of bad Chinese food in the food court, picking at the greasy fried rice and cartilaginous chicken. I was thinking about The Outfit and his threats.

— Sorry about that, I said. He wants our building.

— What? Oh, that guy.

Ah. Maybe he was still focused on that misfired kiss.

I tried to lighten things by asking if we could try a second first date, and although he brightened briefly, he was again lost in thought a moment later. We spent a couple hours walking around the mall, trailed by my worry and his disappointment, making bad small talk and trying to avoid long conversational pauses that would send us back into our own concerns. Still, by the time we emerged into the warm sunlight later that afternoon, he seemed more like himself— at least, more like the guy I barely knew who'd proposed a library first date—which merely served to highlight my own distractedness. At the busy intersection of James and

King, he tried for a second kiss, but the crush of pedestrians at the crosswalk jostled us into a hug instead, all angle and bone. I circled the block twice as I walked back to the apartment, processing the afternoon's conflicting aftertastes, the stale mint of hope for this new thing with The Scarf against the metallic tang of continued uncertainty for my family. He should have walked me home, I thought as I opened our door. Here, that kiss could have connected properly.

A thunderstorm had rocked the city overnight, with record amounts of rain pummelling the humidity into submission. We woke to a downtown that had been scoured clean, yet barely a puddle remained as evidence of the storm.

The new air even put Mom in a better mood. She practically danced through breakfast with Wu on her hip. Her behaviour wasn't a transformation so much as the return of a long-absent loved one. The change was startling, and Leich and I raised our eyebrows at each other. Clearly enjoying the ride, Wu did his best to respond, moving what limbs he could, letting joy out through the impish twinkle in his eye. When he yelled Yay!, even though his facial muscles hadn't recovered enough for a full smile, everyone laughed, even Dad, who'd been sipping his coffee in silence. That laughter, of long release, was better than a cold drink on a hot day.

Leich, Mom, Wu, and I found ourselves in the store in the afternoon, folding, discarding, and refreshing as much as we could after the long humid spell. Leich had stayed after opening to help. Wu was mine for the day, a responsibility for which I had volunteered despite wanting to spend my hours texting a certain boy every time I breathed. Wu kept me busy. His movement was better—he walked around, talking to himself and playing with whatever he found— but he tired easily and needed to be picked up a lot, too.

The humidity had hit the store hard; some of the stock in the storeroom had grown so musty that we had to throw it away. I'd never seen mould grow so quickly—every item of clothing that had been stored against the rear stone wall had grown a coat of white fuzz. The afternoon wore on, and our discard pile grew and grew. Mom, rather than lamenting the ruined stock, simply shrugged when she saw it and went back to her sorting and humming. Leich and I shared another look, this time with a definite sense of hope.

Actually, there were five of us when The Outfit walked in. Not two minutes before, Saul had appeared and commenced rocking on his feet in front of a bookshelf, space pen in one hand, his other migrating south. Leich, nearest the front, was just reaching for the store's cordless to call the group home when The Outfit's two goons came in. This time, there was no pretence of crossed signals about parking—they simply marched in and, like hired bulls in a china shop, started brushing up against things just enough to get them to fall. Right behind them, gliding in on his own shaft of bitter sunlight, The Outfit zeroed in on my mother. He had to pause, though, because Saul blocked the aisle. The goons tried to maneuver close enough to manhandle Saul out of the way but, between the five people already in various spots and their inconvenient bulk, there was nowhere to go without climbing over racks and shelves.

The look The Outfit focused on Saul was pure malice, as though the idea that they were the same species was an affront to the natural order.

— Get out of my way. Now.

Saul was oblivious, supremely focused on the cracked paperback spines in front of him as he continued to rock. The rest of us just watched, almost paralyzed.

— I will not say it again.

Still rocking, Saul turned towards the threatening voice. When he saw The Outfit's face, he changed. I expected him to melt down like he had the last time. However, what flitted into Saul's eyes was anger, so pure and raw that if he had wanted to, he could have thrust that space pen through The Outfit's chest as easily as if the mobster had been made of tinfoil. And then the anger was gone, replaced by a visible urge to flee. He pushed past The Outfit and shuffled as quickly as he could from the store, his eyes on the floor. The Outfit sniffed.

— Such people should never be allowed to be born, he said.

Redness began to creep up my mother's throat to her face, firing up her cheeks. She took a step towards him. The goons saw her but were hemmed in, unable to move. Their eyes were hidden behind their dark glasses, but even their chins looked embarrassed.

— Leave, she said.

The Outfit looked amused.

— Your husband has my papers. Tell him it is time.

— I'll do no such thing. Leich, call the police.

Leich pulled out his phone, dialled 911, and brought the phone to his ear. The Outfit sighed and tilted his head towards my brother. The closest goon, not hesitating this time, barged past me and Wu, knocking us against the wall. He snatched the phone from Leich's ear and ended the call by bringing the handset down onto the counter with a crunch. My brother didn't move, even though he was close enough to be reflected, large and inverted, in the goon's glasses. Leich was angry, I could see, although it was a calm, steady kind, drawn from the same source as the composure shown during the robbery. I'll always remember how he looked in those moments, and how awed by him I was. That was my brother's summer of stepping forward.

The Outfit wagged a finger and tsk-tsked.

— That was unnecessary. You should keep better control of your children, Anne.

My mother, hearing her name used so intimately in concert with the threat against her children, started to move again, her face now crimson. The Outfit sniffed again, adjusted his cufflinks and his pink tie, and stepped out through the front door of the store. His goons followed.

The word for it was fury, pure and simple, of blast-furnace strength. I had never seen—and would never see again—my mother so consumed. Not when Dad left, not when he returned, and never in any of the hundreds of other angry moments she would still have to pass through. Yet her control was complete even as she seemed to glow white-hot—only love can contain that kind of fury.

— Mutton, take Wu upstairs, she said.

— I'm going to finish that call, Leich said.

He went behind the register, muttering under his breath when he realized that the cordless was away from its cradle. He began to root around under the counter. Amidst the rustling and clunking, I heard the grinding of glass on glass as he moved the old sepia photograph out of the way.

— Leich, don't, Mom said. There's no point.

— You heard him, he—

— The police can't do anything.

— But—

— I said no. Mutton, go. There are snacks on the counter for your brother.

Wu, with that clarity of perception small children have, was quiet. I would have expected him to be upset, angry, fussy, scared, or sad, but he wasn't. He was just quiet, like right then he knew it was best to wait. I'd picked him up when The Outfit came in, and he remained perched on my hip, steadfast and still, his tiny hand on my arm, his eyes on my face, as we walked out and turned towards the apartment gate. Mom and Leich's argument faded behind us.

As we left the store, my eyes were drawn to Satan's Falafel across the street. Either The Outfit, having dispensed with the irksome task of threatening our family, had realized how hungry he was, or felt the need to drop more unpleasantness on someone. Likely the second option. One of the goons stepped towards Mr. Ahmad. I expected Mr. Ahmad, like anyone, to step back and prevent himself from being pinched between the hulking man and the falafel cart. He didn't. He just stood right where he was and said a few words to the goon, who stopped cold. I wanted to imagine that Mr. Ahmad simply refused to serve any of them, or that the goon saw something immovable in Mr. Ahmad's eyes. I wanted to imagine that Mr. Ahmad's former life had made him into a man who simply refused to fear The Outfit. I saw the goon actually take a half-step back, flustering all three of them enough to walk away. I'd love to know what Mr. Ahmad said—watching them scurry back to the car was a bright but temporary spot on that day.

My phone rang early, first droning around my dreams like an unseen mosquito, then waking me up with the clashing sounds of my cheery ring tone and the phone's vibrating alert against the wood of the nightstand. I grabbed the phone, excited through my fog that it might be The Scarf. But it was Marvin from the Guild, telling me that Razza's windows had been smashed, and that glass and stuff from the head shop lay strewn all over the sidewalk. He felt bad about calling so early, and apologized in such an impenetrable gush I had to hang up on him so I could wake Dad with the news. Dad was up in a hurry—in his adrenaline-fuelled confusion he almost climbed over Mom to get to the door—and on the phone within minutes, barking at the police and the insurance company with equal strength.

By the time Leich and I went down to open the store, a couple of police cruisers had arrived and the scene was marked off with yellow police tape. A fire truck was also there, adding its flashers to the dancing mess of light in front of the building. The police officers and firemen leaned against the truck, sipping coffees from the Tim Hortons a few doors up from the store. Not doing much of anything, really, just watching my father pace back and forth along the front of the Weston, looking at his BlackBerry as though he was willing someone, anyone, to call.

My first thought was that the crime-scene tape and the emergency response was a bit much for a simple smash-and-grab, but my second was of our robbery, of the gun and the robber's blond hair. Suddenly it didn't seem like overkill at all, and it felt odd that Leich and I had to open the store as though everything were normal, though it clearly wasn't.

Marvin was waiting by the door at Second Chances, rubbing his hands together and watching my father. A young guy in a hoodie and frayed ball cap had lined up right behind him, as though afraid to lose his spot. Marvin took a step towards me.

— I'm so sorry for the early call—

— It's good you did, I said. We might not have known otherwise.

— Crappy way to start a day, I know, but—

— Are you open now?

It was the young guy—a McMaster grad student crunching a summer deadline, judging by the five o'clock shadow and two-handed grip on his dented travel mug—and he looked annoyed at having to wait. Martin did a half-turn and gave him a sharp look of his own.

— In a few minutes, Leich said to the guy.

— I've been here since—

— We've both been waiting, Marvin said. Relax.

The young guy muttered something and went back to squinting at the lid of his mug. I introduced Marvin to Leich.

— Glad you called, Leich said. Glad you were up so early.

— Before dawn, actually, Marvin said. Haven't been up this early in years. Just had the sudden need for a walk, of all things, and found myself here.

Leich thanked Marvin again, unlocked the door, and went inside.

I was about to follow him in when a dull flash of red and blue farther along the front of our building, away from the break-in, caught my eye. The twins were sleeping on long pieces of cardboard wedged at the angle of wall and sidewalk and right at the brick-line between Second Chances and City Bingo. There might be no sadder sight than children sleeping on the street. Despite the hardship of sleeping outside, on night-cooled concrete, their faces were peaceful. Maybe they were enjoying dreams that took them far away from the filthy sidewalks. I hoped so, anyhow.

— Amazing what a person can sleep through, Marvin said.

— The cops haven't bothered them, I said. That's surprising.

— Humanity from our boys in black—will wonders never cease, eh?

I went inside to help Leich set up. Leich was tapping away on his phone in front of the cash register when I brought out the Niche item, a small pendant made of black stone hung on a long silver chain. The stone, perhaps two inches long, had been carved with grooves that seemed to swirl upwards. The longer I looked at it, the more it seemed to move, like it was trying to fly.

I waited.

— Nice, he said when he finally looked up.

— That's it? 'Nice'?

He shrugged and went back to his phone, his thumbs a blur. I found a free space on one of the shelves.

— I guess I'm doing this all by myself today, I said in Leich's direction.

Still no response.

I swung open the door and stepped onto the sidewalk, seating the latches and bolts into their unlocked positions.

Marvin and the younger guy—Travel Mug, I decided his name would be—went by me into Second Chances. I looked over at Razza's. The scene was calmer: only the police car parked right in front of the shop still had its lights flashing and the firefighters were moving around their truck, looking ready to leave. The other police cruiser turned off its lights and merged into the trickle of vehicles moving past the emergency obstruction. With his BlackBerry glued to one ear, Dad watched it go, scowling. I gave him a wave but he didn't see me.

Back in the store, Marvin and Travel Mug were arguing beside one of the shelves. Travel Mug had blocked the narrow aisle, obstructing Marvin's path to the front. They were arguing over the Niche item, which Marvin held in one hand. The other was raised, as though pushing at the invisible wall of air between him and Travel Mug.

— Move, Marvin said.

— But I saw it first, Travel Mug said.

— I already had it in my hand by the time you came over.

— You saw me looking at it, then you grabbed it.

— Bullshit. I came right here.

It was a rare thing, but every now and again a couple of customers would squabble over an item in the store. But this was the first time I'd seen two grown men ready to exchange blows. Travel Mug was at the disadvantage. He wasn't a small guy, but even I could see that Marvin had more experience behind him. I knew him as a crusty-but-kind thriller writer, but his long grey beard, black jeans, Guns N' Roses T-shirt, and black leather vest suggested a grittiness that the younger guy couldn't match. They argued about the item back and forth even though Marvin was in control, and the tension rose.

And I'd never encountered conflict over a Niche item. It was odd that thinking about it made me unable to move or do anything about the fight brewing in Second Chances. Just when the first blows seemed inevitable, Leich's voice rose above the squabble.

— Who's holding it?

He'd appeared in the aisle behind Travel Mug, forcing him to turn away from Marvin to acknowledge the question. The two men stopped arguing.

— It was right there, and I—

— Who's holding it? Leich asked again.

— He is.

— Did you ever even get a hand on it?

— No.

— So what's the problem? He got to it first, he gets to buy it. Simple.

Marvin watched without comment, a slight smile pulling at the corner of his mouth. Travel Mug threw up a frustrated hand and wandered to the back of the store, muttering under his breath. He stopped in front of an old leather letterman jacket, took it from the rack, and distracted himself with trying it on. Leich's phone chimed in his pocket and it was in his hand before the end of the second alert. He grinned at the screen and began tapping out a response as he moved towards the front door.

— You all right, Mutts?

The question was tossed over his shoulder like an afterthought.

— I suppose so—hey, will you check in on Dad? He—

— Great. Later.

And he was gone, leaving me in the store with the two guys for company. Marvin came to the register holding the pendant, looking down at it with something akin to love.

— First thing I saw, he said.

— Three dollars, I said.

— What? No way, that's not enough.

I laughed and started to rib him about not knowing how to bargain, but the protest must have come from somewhere deep in his subconscious, because he handed over a five-dollar bill without further comment and walked straight out without waiting for his change. I called after him before realizing how silly I must have looked. I rang the toonie back into the till, thinking I'd give it to him at the next Guild meeting.

I'd managed to ignore my own phone, which had been mostly silent until a few minutes before and was now buzzing every few seconds. The Scarf must have slept in, settling into his texting as his groggy head cleared. After a dozen texts or so, I was interrupted. The student came up with the jacket, clearly taken by its perfectly worn leather. But the price, which we thought was fair given the shape it was in, was a little higher than most people were comfortable paying in a thrift store. No one had even bargained for it, which was unusual: people often have a deep need and love for haggling in thrift stores. He put it on the counter and sipped from the travel mug. He smelled like burnt coffee.

— I don't have enough on me. Can you hold it for me until I can pay?

I nodded, slid my phone away, and took the jacket behind the counter.

— Thanks, he said.

I asked him how he'd heard about the store. He pulled out his phone and showed me the store's page on the blue and white Facebook app, saying how it was being shared all over campus news feeds. His face had relaxed since his encounter with Marvin. Eventually, he walked out and I returned the jacket to its place on the rack. He hadn't said when he would be back to claim it, nor had I asked—you can sense when people say things to save face.

I learned the details of the break-in at Razza's later that morning after Dad was finished with the cops. I was texting with The Scarf when he came in and I hid my phone, blushing. Dad didn't notice and launched into it. Someone had broken the glass on Razza's front door and defeated the lock with a drill before going inside. All the shelves and racks had been overturned, the display cases smashed, the stock of water pipes and other paraphernalia destroyed. What hadn't been destroyed outright had been sprayed with the store's fire extinguishers, soaking the clothing and magazines and frosting everything else with a haze of foam. But nothing had been stolen, not even the newish flat-screen TV on the wall, the cash register, or the new stock still in boxes in the back. The safe was untouched too.

— The liquidators were supposed to come today for his stock, Dad said, shaking his head.

— Nothing was taken? I asked.

— No. Just ruined.

— That seems so harsh.

— The creditors can't even get their inventory back.

Dad had to be thinking about the break-in as another less-than-subtle message from The Outfit—I knew I was. It wasn't as though it had been a drunken smash-and-grab. No, whoever had broken in would've made a lot of noise breaking in and spent significant time ransacking the store. Razza had assured my father that he had set and armed the security system. The police had said no one had filed a complaint about an alarm going off that night, so whomever had done this was skilled enough to defeat a relatively new system. That meant organization.

— Oh, and Mutton? Thanks for letting me have those few days. Sometimes—

He paused, thinking.

— Sometimes it takes a while to say things in the best way, he said.

Yes, it does. I knew that feeling very well.

— You're welcome, Dad.

Mom came by with Wu a few minutes later so Dad repeated the story for her. I watched them as they talked, Dad looking worn out about the whole thing and Mom becoming more stressed as he spoke. Yet her voice, when she asked questions, was level and calm, and she managed to draw strength from his answers, even though she must have reached the same conclusions about why Razza's had been ransacked. Eventually, Dad checked his watch and said he had a meeting to get to. He kissed her and Wu goodbye and winked at me as he left. As Mom puttered around the cash register, I told her about Marvin and Travel Mug's argument over the Niche item and how easily Leich had defused the situation. She was interested in the pendant, and I was surprised to hear myself describing the item, how it seemed to soar all on its own. I'd expected her to get upset at Leich stepping into the argument—taking any risk so soon after the robbery—but she even seemed to relax a little.

The door opened. The same cop who had worked with us after the robbery walked in, looking as puffed up as ever, squinting as his eyes adjusted to the light. Mom's calm disappeared. I could practically hear her tension popping like old springs under new weight.

— I just wanted to make sure that you ladies were all right.

How could one person generate so much irritation? He actually sauntered towards us with one hand on the butt of his gun and the other on the other side of his Batman belt, showing off the smoothness he was issued along with his badge.

— Not now, officer, she said with remarkable restraint.

— Oh, come now. It's a free service we provide.

An image of my mother popping the cop in the mouth with a quick right jab flashed into my mind, catching me off guard. It shouldn't have been funny, but it was. I laughed, quick and sharp, out before I could wrestle it back behind my teeth. He gave an exaggerated frown, as though his feelings had been wounded, but I managed to bite back the even more inappropriate response to that expression. My mother looked at me with something like pride— Brava, kiddo, for getting it out first, the look seemed to say—before pelting him with enough questions about our robbery investigation to knock him off balance. His answers didn't satisfy, either, which just made her dig deeper.

After a while, it became clear that she wasn't going to let up. It was also clear that I wasn't expected to participate, so to keep myself from laughing more at the beleaguered police officer I tuned them out and pulled out my phone. I'd missed a bunch of messages since I checked last, double the volume, as though The Scarf had finally warmed up, his nimble hands becoming faster throughout the morning.

I was distracted from the phone's screen by a dark shape appearing in front of the shop's glass door. Close enough to cast a shadow on the dirty glass—hadn't I just washed it not too long before?—but too far away to reveal who it was. The shadow drew nearer, hesitant, like it was debating whether or not to come in. There was a flash of blond hair as the door opened. He was inside before I could open my mouth, although what would I have said? Mom, Mr. Police Officer, the guy who robbed us and shot up the store is back? My insides are liquefying? Is he still armed and dangerous? Isn't the cop armed and dangerous, too? What would have come out would have probably sounded like someone screaming as they drowned. Mom and the cop turned their heads as the motion caught their peripheral vision, but went back to their game of questions. And why wouldn't they? They hadn't been there, hadn't seen the bright hair and the pale skin, the big black hole that had threatened to swallow Leich and me.

But the blond robber had changed. At the time, the robbery had filled him with a panicked sense of purpose, but the man who now stood in front of me, eyes to the floor, sallow face drawn, clothing so loose it was pooling around his ankles, was not the same guy. Even though it clearly was. He looked beaten. Hollowed out like a grave.

He reached into his pocket and looked at me. As his eyes met mine, my insides spasmed. But there was no gun. Instead, he took a little silver box from the pocket with impossible care and laid it on the counter. It gleamed, every carving on every side shining as though it had been hand-polished.

— I'm sorry—

His voice cut off in the middle of a wavering note and he swallowed, his Adam's apple rising and falling.

— I think this belongs to someone else, he managed.

Mom and the police officer, facing away from us, finally stopped talking. Maybe it was the warped intensity of his voice or the genuineness of his apology. Maybe they heard him letting go of something he had held too long. I certainly saw him let go. He fell to his knees and pulled the gun from the other pocket. The same gun. I nearly wet myself again. My mother's mouth opened. The cop hesitated an instant before drawing his gun and aiming it at the man's chest. The man paused and set the small pistol on the floor beside him. He shuddered, raised his eyes to the ceiling, laid his hands on his thighs, and waited.

The cop barked into his radio, yelled at the guy to get down and lace his fingers together behind his head, and cuffed him on the ground, wrenching his arms one at a time behind his back. A few moments later, the sound of rising sirens and squealing tires filled the street out front, the windows flashed blue and red, red and blue, and the store was filled with noise and motion. My mother and I were hustled outside and down the street. More officers arrived and fanned out around the scene, their movements quick and jarring. As the officers dragged the blond guy out and tucked him into the back of a cruiser, his face, despite the tense situation, looked calm.

Released, I thought. He looks released.

It had been a long, long day. For the obvious reasons, of course, like the police follow-up to the robber's unexpected surrender, bagging the gun and interviewing Mom and me, asking about further charges, signing statements, and so on. Dad, again berating himself for being absent during his family's time of need, paced around the store until an officer had to ask him to find a chair.

But somehow I moved away from all of that and towards the predictable. Like a cloned, mechanical version of myself—Mutton 2.0, with standard firmware, nicknamed Girl in Love—my boy-struck body, emotions, and mind conspired against my reasonable self. Even as the other tumultuous events in my life gathered speed like runaway trains on downhill grades, I couldn't escape love for long. Or what passes for love at fifteen, anyhow, the breathless anticipation you feel after an awkward first kiss, the idealized magic you call destiny, the held hands and perfect shared looks you envision defining your next encounter. I was back on my phone the moment I was no longer needed at the store, only to find that the last text in my inbox had arrived at the moment the robber reappeared. After that, nothing. I sent a flurry of new messages but received no replies.

The Scarf and I hadn't seen each other since our first date, but that wasn't enough to keep me from thinking about and texting him. A lot. But we were tethered only by the text messages burning up the ether between our phones, and now even that had been interrupted. I tried calling, even, only to find myself routed to his voicemail which he, like everyone else my age, never checked.

What is it about anticipation that makes it so difficult to deal with?

The evening had arrived, dinner had been consumed and cleaned up, and my family had dispersed to our various nighttime activities. Hours later I was still waiting, alone in the living room, driving myself crazy with the thoughts a girl has when expected contact doesn't materialize. There were a few moments where I imagined running down to the street to flag down passing taxis, barking at the poor drivers up and down the city streets, cruising Hamilton looking for him. I even thought about bumbling around on city buses and their finely delineated, predictable, desperate routes.

My journal sat open in my lap, the page cold and empty apart from a few angry doodles and frustrated first lines. I had all this great material, was being filled and filled and filled, but couldn't release it onto the page. I threw the book across the living room and then, in a fit of guilt, went over to it to make sure it was all right. I groaned and sank back onto the couch.

— This isn't me, I said. Too girly, right?

The empty living room didn't answer.

To give my hands something to do, I grabbed an apple from the fruit bowl. It was mealy, like it had been sitting too long, and I ended up spitting it into a tissue. They talk about the intersection of life and love as being a roller coaster, but on a roller coaster you never had to wonder where you would end up. My life was probably more like riding a pogo stick, one of the creaky, rusty ones from way back when, where every hop threatened to send you into a hedge. Where stepping off to save yourself was even more scary than riding it out.

Leich came out of his room a few minutes later. He was dressed in a clean collared shirt and dark jeans, and I might have smelled a hint of cologne. But he looked tired.

— I still can't believe you waited until dinner to tell me about the guy coming back, he said.

— We didn't think about it, I said. Besides, you weren't really around, you know?

— That's what cell phones are for, Mutts.

— They work both ways, big brother.

— I should have been there.

— Having fewer people there was probably better.

— I don't get it—he just walked in and gave himself up?

— Like he knew there was a cop in there, ready with handcuffs. Like it was convenient.

— What about Mom?

— Scared, but she didn't see anything until the end.

— And you?

I paused.

— You're not telling me something, he said.

— There's nothing to hide. Except—

— Except what?

— The silver box—the Niche thing—was perfectly clean and polished, I said.

— So?

— Like he'd taken care of it since the robbery.

— You can't possibly know that.

— I know. But I kind of do.

Leich tilted his head and gave me a skeptical look.

— I know, I know, I said. Crazy, right?

— As I said before—how are *you* doing?

His tone, both concerned and mocking, reminded me of how irrational I must have sounded. Leich watched me for a few moments, waiting for a response, and I began fidgeting with the journal in my lap. Open. Closed. Open. Closed. I could have given him a more revealing answer to the concerned part of his question, but I didn't, latching instead onto my own self-consciousness. Besides, there was no telling how he'd respond to a full dose of honesty: that I was as concerned about somehow getting a second kiss as I was about the robber's bizarre return and arrest. A big brother would have a field day with that kind of admission. No way that was happening.

— Fine, I said.

— You sure?

— Yes.

— Okay.

He pulled out his phone and grinned into the darkened screen, checking his teeth. A notification arrived, lighting up his face in a bluish glow. He pocketed the device and looked at the apartment door. It was a Friday night, so he was going out, I supposed, which would leave me alone in the apartment—apart from Wu sleeping in his room, my quiet phone, and my writing that wasn't quite getting done. Leich dropped the hissing baby monitor—which my parents refused to retire, even though Wu had his own bed and no longer needed watching—onto the couch beside me.

— You're on Wu duty, he said.

— I guess so, I said.

I was annoyed that he had plans, leaving me again to babysit, and that I had no cause to argue otherwise.

To stall him, I almost revisited our family's dinner conversation. Although the state would be laying charges for the robbery and weapons offences, we had the option of pursuing damages for the assault and emotional trauma of the event. In the end we decided that we would support the police case against him, but that civil litigation would only add layers of difficulty and expense for us, and drain more from the robber than he had to give. The family taking it in stride wasn't as surprising as it might have been if the summer hadn't already thrown the works at us. My boy-distraction helped take my mind off it as well. After the family meeting—which was remarkably brief—Mom and Dad went out to a dinner thrown by the downtown business owners' association. They were likely facing not only small talk and schmoozing—which they hated—but also the inevitable questions from the other business owners about all the crazy things happening at Second Chances. They had left the apartment holding hands.

I picked up the monitor and looked at the hazy, black and white screen. I could just make out one of Wu's feet—he'd taken to balling himself up at the head of the bed to sleep. I turned up the volume; the scratchy rhythms of Wu's gentle snoring filled the living room. A comforting sound.

No, I thought, there's no need to keep Leich from enjoying his evening.

— So where are you going? I asked.

— Out.

— Out where?

— Just out.

My phone thrummed in my pocket. I had it out, heart in my throat, before the text tone had even finished. It was just Peter.

— *I heard about what happened. How are you doing?*

Such precise construction; Peter was adamant about proper spelling and punctuation, even in e-communications. Disappointed, I turned off the screen and put the phone away. I could call him any time.

While I was checking my message, Leich had wandered into the kitchen. He'd located a leftover slice of cake and was trying to polish it off in a single bite. He tried to speak around the masticated mass of brown in his mouth, but I held up a hand.

— I'll wait, I said.

He swallowed with a mighty gulp and began picking at his teeth.

— What happened to the silver box?

— I put it back on to the shelf, I said.

— Funny that the cop didn't take it as evidence.

— It was like he didn't even see it, even though it was right next to the gun.

At the mention of the gun, a brief shadow flashed across my brother's features. But he recovered quickly, smiling extra wide to display the disgusting brown flecks between his teeth—brothers are brothers are brothers, after all. Pulling out his phone, he texted as he walked back down the hall to the bathroom. The sound of his electric tooth-brush hummed through the bathroom door—he didn't want chocolate bits in his teeth wherever he was going. His footfalls were heavy as he walked out—he and Dad shared that trait, neither had the capacity to walk softly—leaving me in the empty apartment.

I checked my phone. Still nothing.

I snatched the remote control and turned on our small TV. We didn't have cable, just a limited selection of broadcast channels we picked up with the antenna on the roof—on post-hippie principle, Dad refused to pay the cable companies—so I channel surfed a while, watching bits here and there. A fight scene in an old Technicolor movie. A few minutes of a hockey game. About thirty seconds of a sitcom with a depressing, canned laugh track. I switched back to the movie, where the two men who had been fighting had apparently reconciled, and were leading a mob to storm the gates of a large prison with stones and Molotov cocktails.

Some time later, the buzzing of my phone on the coffee table woke me. I shook my head and stretched, feeling foggy. There was a new movie on now, a recent thriller with lots of gunplay, car chases, and bad dialogue; the clock on the DVD player told me I had slept for more than two hours. Blinking away the haze, I grabbed the phone, think-ing I should probably text Peter to let him know that I was all right. No, I thought as I yawned and stretched again, I should probably call. The phone buzzed again in my hand as a second message arrived.

— *IM SORRY*, read the message preview.

The message preview said that it was The Scarf. Excited and also a little puzzled about the apology, I opened my inbox to read his previous message.

— *WE SHUD JUST B FRENDS*

I must have read it a hundred times, no exaggeration, with each reading bringing a new feeling. The tastelessness of breaking up by text message. Anger at his cowardice. Embarrassment of having cared only to be let down. That I was a living cliché worthy of teen romance novels and careless gossip. But more than any of those things, and what I remember first even now when I think about that night, was wondering if he even knew that he had ended things between us with a yell. That the messages, written all in capital letters, were received by a girl who had already been threatened too many times that summer and would agonize, even when her head knew better, about whether she had somehow caused him to yell at her.

Leich got home about thirty minutes after the second text message. He smelled like onions and barbecue, like he'd spent the evening at one of those chain restaurants with mediocre food and questionable service. He plopped himself down on the couch beside me, snatched the remote, and began flipping through channels. I hadn't cried yet—I wouldn't cry until a few days later for an event of even greater magnitude—but was still stunned.

He looked at me.

— What's wrong with you?

His breath smelled slightly sweet and sour.

— You've been drinking, I said.

A bashful look before reclaiming his cool.

— Yeah, a glass of wine with dinner.

— You have to brush your teeth. Mom and Dad will crucify you.

The distraction was welcome, actually, and it felt good to drop guilt on my brother, to be the pesky little sister again. He was surprised at the suggestion, and suspicious, as though there were other motives at play other than sibling solidarity. And a glass of wine? Not a beer, or one of those other strong drinks that are supposed to make a guy more of a guy? Intriguing. He jumped off the couch and when he returned a few minutes later, conspicuously minty, he resumed his passive channel surfing.

— How's Wu?

— Still sleeping, I suppose. Haven't heard a peep.

— So, like I said, what's wrong?

I said nothing. He snorted and turned off the TV.

— You never spend more than twenty minutes in front of this thing. What's up?

There was the briefest of hesitations, and out it came. All of it, from the first meeting and conversation at Duster's to the kiss in front of that amazing book to the text message dumping I had endured that very evening. Leich just listened. When I wrapped up, holding my phone in both hands like I could wring something more out of it, he stared at me.

— So, this is all less than a week old.

I nodded, readying myself for the inevitable big brother response. Laughter at how ridiculous I was being. Advice to go slow next time. Post-relationship support chestnuts like Time Heals All Wounds or You'll Get Over It or It's His

Loss. But my brother didn't say any of those things. He just sighed, sat back on the couch, and shook his head.

— That's shitty, Mutts. I'm sorry.

If I was going to cry, it would have been then. Not from the heartache but from his unconditional expression of support that didn't try to diminish what I felt. What a wonderful thing for him to say. But I didn't get the chance. When Mom and Dad came up the stairs, surprised and happy to see their two eldest children waiting for them, I decided not to say anything, instead bidding my family goodnight and retreating to my room.

I t felt like I hadn't slept at all. That had never happened to me before. I just lay there and stared into the darkness, going over what I thought had happened—again and again. Being dumped is like grieving. You go through the same stages—shock, disbelief, anger, denial, and so on— plus you get the added bonus of wondering where things went wrong and asking yourself if things could be remedied for the future. With grieving, at least, you have the certainty that the person is gone and that healing is the next step. You're not going to run into the deceased at the library or have to read his stories in your writer's group or worry about chance encounters in a compressed downtown.

By the time I heard the rest of the family stirring to begin their Saturday, I felt sick to my stomach, the emotional hit conspiring with the lack of sleep to tie my insides into tight little pretzels. I had never been particularly worried about boys or finding a boyfriend. I didn't have anything against boys, I just didn't think about them much. And now in one short stretch of summer, I had double trouble on the boy front. Peter's gentle way of letting me know how he felt contrasted sharply with the library kiss and dizzy texting rush that had consumed me for the past few days.

I stood, threw on some clothes, and went across the hall to the bathroom. The echoes from the animated voices of my family tumbled like acrobats down the hall; walking through them felt like interrupting a performance. I recognized the face staring back at me in the mirror, but it felt like a pathetic disguise. I splashed water onto my face, but it just made me wet and cold and slightly more alert. I dropped my jeans to the floor and sat on the toilet, peeing desultorily and zoning out as the cold seat warmed beneath me.

A knock.

— Mutton, breakfast is ready, my mother said through the door.

— Okay, Mom.

— We're waiting for you.

— No, don't. I'll be out in a bit. Go ahead.

Breakfast was ready? They were waiting? Now, our family did the family thing as much as we could, but rarely around a sit-down breakfast; a communal breakfast on a Saturday was almost unheard of. I had been counting on the normal dynamic to hide that all wasn't right for me.

The two shadows of Mom's feet beneath the door lingered a few moments, but left eventually. I stood up, kicked my pants away, took off my shirt and underwear, and assessed the damage in the full-length mirror behind the door. Everything was fine, apart from the dark fatigue under my eyes. The same mousy-haired teenager stood there, her body pale and slim, the expected teenage developments progressing on schedule. The mirror was slightly warped, so it made me look thinner than I actually was. I made some facial expressions and threw a few slinky poses, watching how my muscles moved with me, trying to see if there was anything amiss.

All looked normal; I was almost disappointed.

But you can't see a broken heart, can you? It aches,

moves deeper with every breath. I stepped into the tub and ran the shower as hot as I could stand, letting the needles of heat on my head and shoulders and chest distract me from, well, everything.

— Yay, Mutton!

That kid's smile could knock down walls and draw a grin even from his heartbroken sister. He held out his arms, wanting to be swept into play, but I saw from the mess on his plate that he wasn't finished eating. I grabbed his elbows, well clear of the mushy cereal on his hands, and planted a kiss on the only clean spot on his forehead.

— Maybe later, bud, I said.

— Okay, he said, returning his attention to his meal.

Mom was sitting at the table with her iPad, reading the news and sipping an improbably large mug of coffee. The shower, not part of my usual pre-breakfast routine, had felt great, the steam and hot water heating my skin to a pleasant pink glow. I sat and ran a wooden comb through my hair, squeezing out a few droplets that soaked themselves into dark grey dimes on my shoulders.

— Feel better?

My mom was studying me.

— A bit, thanks. How did you know?

— Leich was worried about you.

I didn't feel as betrayed as you might expect. Despite my independence and introverted ways, one of the conclusions I had reached overnight was that this new thing might be too much to handle on my own. I hated the idea of reaching out, worried about the things you worry about when you admit vulnerability. I put the comb down on the table and poured some shredded wheat into a bowl. Not because I was hungry, but maybe something like cereal could absorb whatever acid was eating away at my insides.

— He opened for you today, she said.

I started to apologize, but she waved it off.

— Do you want to talk about it?

No, not really. And yes, I did. I sighed.

Before I could answer, the cordless phone rang. I leaned back in my chair and plucked it from its cradle. Leich was calling from downstairs. Strange thing, speaking by phone to someone under your feet, the voice through the floor pulling at the delayed version on the handset.

— Thanks for opening. I—

— Can you come down? I, um, haven't—look, can you?

His voice was flat, like he was trying to stay calm.

— What's up?

He laughed, a tight, strained noise.

— Just come down.

So I did, dashing to my room, grabbing my phone, slipping on my flip-flops, and heading for the door. Mom rose from the table, looking concerned, but I told her not to worry. She said to call if we needed anything. When I got to the sidewalk, a young couple was just leaving the store, carrying retro clothing in the old grocery bags we repurposed for the task. As I opened the door, I couldn't believe my eyes: Second Chances was full of people, at least fifteen or twenty. It doesn't sound like much, but the store was so small it looked full. Leich was behind the counter watching the store bustle around him, stunned. When he saw me he just motioned with both hands at the milling people as if to say, see why I called?

— When did they get here?

— They were waiting when I came down.

— Wow. This is—

— It scared me a little, actually. I almost called the police. Who lines up in front of a second-hand store before eight on a Saturday?

— Have any of them said anything about why they came?

— Not to me, but I've overheard a few people saying they just ended up here.

— I've heard that a few times, too.

— Our Facebook page? Twitter?

— So many, so soon?

— No, you're right. Unlikely.

We watched the crowd for a few moments. It was a lovely demographic representation of Hamilton, actually. There were a couple of guys in safety boots looking at DVDs. An old woman and her granddaughter were checking out the picture books. A young woman in a hijab was sitting in front of the bookshelf, reading a copy of Dante's *Inferno* we'd had for a couple of years. There was a girlish squeal of delight from the cramped, curtained change room in the corner. A few people picked through the knick-knacks while others flipped through the racks of clothes. There was even a teenage boy, one of the goths from my school, holding up a pair of crystal candleholders, appraising them with a comically delicate eye. A tall, thin black man with a faded army surplus jacket thanked us as he left.

— I was afraid not to let them in, Leich whispered.

— The Niche item?

— Gone, first thing. A little jade beetle. I think a Ticat player bought it. He was huge.

Then my brother, my ever-so-cool teenage brother, uttered a breathy, nervous giggle. Not a bad nervousness, mind you, more like the nerves that reveal themselves just before a big event. A little manic, but good manic. I envied him, to be honest—the dull gnawing in my stomach had prevented me from being carried away by the moment like he had. I waited for him to ask how I was feeling, but he just stared at the crowd.

— Do you need me to stay?

He answered without looking at me.

— No, I think it'll be fine, he said. I just wanted you to see this.

At the eastern end of Gore Park, a couple of old cannons stood guard, cold, hard sentinels that spoke of a simpler time when enemies were obvious, alliances clear. I imagine they're still there, pointing along King like an invasion from Stoney Creek might be imminent. The statue above them, a weepy tribute to Sir John A., has moved a few times and has been a part of Hamilton's downtown lore for over a hundred years. But those cannons are a mystery to me. How far had they travelled? Had they ever been fired? I've set a number of my stories right there in that park and have created worlds around that monument. But the truth behind those cannons? I have no idea.

Wu loved them. He didn't care about their history or their pedigree or whether they had defended our shores; he'd run around the monument's granite base oohing and hhing and yelling, boom! Boom! Boom! I'd lift him up and he would climb all over, sitting astride them and imagining himself riding into battle against conjured foes. He'd lay his head against the cold iron for minutes at a time, his wrinkled cheek taking on the subtle texture of the ancient metal, listening to the park and traffic sounds, imagining who knows what.

Later that day, I took Wu out to the cannons. It had been a simple thing to volunteer to babysit. Yes, I used my baby brother as a salve for my pain—he always made me feel better, so why not? But he wasn't entirely himself. When we got to the end of the park and he saw the cannons, he smiled, but didn't demand to be taken out of the stroller. He had a lovely sparkle in his eyes as he stared at the statue and the big guns, and part of me knew that he should have been laughing and climbing and pretending. In the end, the outing made me feel worse.

Looking at the cannons wouldn't hold his attention forever so we walked around the park. Mr. Ahmad gave Wu some stale flatbread and we fed the pigeons next to the fountain, making them surge and mutter towards the pieces we threw. A few of the rough downtown dwellers who liked to drive their Rascals to the park for communal smoking sessions gave Wu odd looks as we wheeled by. Jenny and Bart, enjoying a smoke break on Duster's empty patio, waved at us.

My phone thrummed against my hip.

— *Hey, Stranger! :) Where are you? How are you doing?*

I had forgotten to text Peter back.

— *in the prk. i have wu.*

— *I'll be there in 5!*

Gore Park's not that big, so he found us easily. I had located a free bench near our end of the park and sat with my feet stretched out and my arms across the back. Wu was asleep in the stroller and rested peacefully, small and fragile, like an infant bird in a big nest. He should have outgrown that stroller by now, I knew. Peter limped up, sans crutches, a big smile on his face. There was a bit of sawdust in his hair and a smudge of dried glue on his jawline.

— Doc said I should try walking, he said. I tried sitting down to do some work on the cathedral, but I couldn't sit still.

— That's great, Peter.

— I heard about the robber guy turning himself in. Crazy, eh?

— Yeah.

— You all right?

Wu twitched hard enough to momentarily wake himself up. He stretched, his deep-set eyes heavy and only half open, and looked at Peter, who gave him a quick wave. Wu beamed at him, big and trusting, before falling back asleep. I should have said that I was fine and changed the subject, but that didn't happen. Instead, seeing how easily my baby brother and my best friend had fallen into the familiar, how easy and good it was to be around each other, my sadness reared up and bit me in my most tender places.

Peter saw this and sat down.

— What's wrong?

I didn't have the words, so I turned on my phone and showed him The Scarf's messages, not realizing that although it was apparent that someone had broken up with me, he would have no idea who it was. Not anticipating that this new story, one that involved another boy and a relationship he hadn't known about, and finding out not two hundred feet from where he'd shared his own feelings, would land poorly.

He jumped to his feet, gritting his teeth.

— What is this?

I waited for him to express how sorry he was, to reach out with the unconditional acceptance and support I was accustomed to. That I took for granted.

— Who is he?

— I don't know what happened, I said. It was so good and fun and when he kissed me and I thought—

— He *kissed* you?

And I barrelled on. I was asleep with my mouth open and running.

— So now I'm dumped, I said. What should I do?

— I can't believe this. You want *my* advice?

— Of course. You're my best—

Then I remembered. Right then. I wanted to slap myself.

— God, Peter, I'm sorry, I said.

Peter left. Of course he did. But not before he laid into me. With angry words and accusations of insensitivity, all deserved. I let him get it out, feeling as small as a period on a very big page. For a moment, anyhow. Don't mistake my extended silence for sensitivity or sacrifice— no, self-preservation has a way of stealing even moments of shame—because by the time he finished, I was again distracted by how I had been feeling before he arrived. By the time he limped away, hurt and fuming, I might not have been thinking of his feelings at all.

Around our household, Sundays had always been a favourite day. Not having to open the store by eight was a delicious luxury. Sundays felt so out of the ordinary that I always imagined them as days on their own, detached from the week by their freedom. The unspoken rule was that we could do as we pleased. Typically, I'd sleep in and eat a leisurely breakfast, enjoying the glow of the unscheduled day ahead of me. Even Mom got into the spirit, avoiding anything to do with Second Chances. Leich could sleep like no person I'd ever known; we'd sometimes have to wake him up in the afternoon just to make sure he was still alive.

I'm not sure I would have done anything differently if I'd known that Sunday was the last one we'd enjoy before everything changed. Maybe I would have tried to stay in bed longer or been more intentional about spending extra time with my brothers and parents.

I opened the windows, letting in fresh air unhindered by the usual city sounds. Hamilton stopped on Sunday mornings. Later, churchgoers would head out and a few cars would scuttle here and there on errands and visits, but that early it was as quiet as a long, deep breath. I looked out the kitchen window and across the street. Gore Park was wreathed in morning shadows, empty and calm. Even Satan's Falafel took the morning off.

I debated whether or not to text an apology to Peter. I should have called, I knew, given how thoroughly I'd been stung by text messages in the recent past, but it was hard to imagine what to say. How poorly I had treated him, how selfish I'd been, had finally occurred to me in the smallest hours of the morning. But it was still way too early. He wouldn't have minded, but my avoidance of conflict won the argument.

I loaded up some toast with thick layers of peanut butter and jam, tucked my journal under my arm, and went to the couch. I clicked open my pen and turned to the next blank page, writing and underlining the date at the top left, as was my custom. Part of my Sunday ritual was hitting the journal. Sundays often birthed many of my best stories. Not this one, though. The date and the thick scrawl beneath stared at me for a long while.

I didn't get much done.

Eventually, the rest of the house started moving. Dad walked into the kitchen carrying Wu, managing with one hand to get a pot of coffee going. While the machine spit and moaned, he came into the living room, plunked my groggy brother down with some toy cars on the rug, and sat at the opposite end of the couch, staring at nothing. Useless before that first cup. Mom came in next, her bright yoga outfit clashing with her bleary expression. She grabbed her iPad, chugged a glass of water, and headed towards the den and her rolled up exercise mat. A moment later, Dad got up to get the milk and sugar ready for when the coffee maker's last gasp and half-hearted beep signalled that all was ready. He handed me a full mug and sat back down.

— One regular coffee, as ordered.

I hadn't ordered it, of course, and rarely drank coffee, but its warmth felt nice in my hands. Wu pushed himself up and walked over to us. He held a tiny red car out for me, nodded soberly when I took it, and went over to the toy box, engrossed in his play-world. Dad chuckled and blew on his coffee.

— He just assumes you're part of the game, he said.

— Like I need a job or something.

— Wouldn't it be great if a few toy cars could make the world disappear for us, too?

— Reality, though—

— Yeah, he said. Reality.

We sat and sipped for a few moments.

— How's the writing going these days?

Not expected. There was a gaping hole in my memory around the last time he had expressed interest in my writing. Had he said a thing about it since he came back to us? He must have—he was so encouraging—but a concrete recollection eluded me.

— Not very well, I admitted, holding up the empty page.

— Hard to create when you're so distracted, I imagine.

— It's just a toy—

— I think you know that I'm not talking about Wu's car.

So he knew, too. Wonderful.

— Really hard, I said. Impossible, actually.

— You'll get it back.

— All it takes is time—

— Ah. So you've heard that one, have you?

Sure I have, I thought. But it's never been said to me.

He smiled into his mug but didn't press any further. Good. I had zero desire to talk about boy troubles with my father.

We sat for a few moments in silence. It's fascinating to watch kids get lost in play, how completely they pretend and create. Wu had dug to the bottom of the toy box for some building blocks, arranging them on his mat in a pattern that looked vaguely familiar. I asked him what he was making. He didn't say anything, just pointed at the floor and carried on.

— It's the store, Dad said, laughing.

Wu gave him one big nod and continued to line up the blocks into abstract parts of the store, talking quietly to himself. There was the counter and till. The clothing racks. The shelves. He started building a structure at the back with Duplo blocks, and another behind the first. The storeroom, I thought. When that was done, he grabbed his Duplo people and moved them around, mumbling imaginary Duplo conversations. Two of the figures were moved to the back room and back to the front, and Wu pointed at the first wall he had built with his skinny little forefinger and flexed his thumb.

— Bang, he said.

And just like that, the magic vanished. Oh, the things children absorb, the tragedies they feel and express. Dad and I watched, speechless, as Wu innocently transitioned his people and cars and blocks into a happy new game moments after they had been robbed at gunpoint.

An hour or so later, Mom came into the kitchen wearing a nice light summer top and skirt and declared that we should go to church. Shocked at her put-together appearance and crazy suggestion, we stopped what we were doing and stared at her like an alien had invaded our home. We were not a spiritual bunch. We for sure did not do church.

— Church? Dad asked.

— It's a beautiful day, she said, fixing him with a look. I think we should do something as a family.

Which was exactly what the rest of us had been doing. Dad and Wu had been building an impressive tower with the interlocking Duplo blocks. A teetering masterpiece. Dad was spending as much time building as keeping Wu— delirious with anticipation and looking like he was ready to knock the thing down himself—away from the tower. Leich had gotten up earlier than usual for a Sunday and was sitting at the kitchen table with his laptop. I had given up on writing and was lying on the couch, again neck-deep in *A Boy of Good Breeding*.

Dad recovered from his initial shock, and stood.

— All right, we can do that. Kids, let's get moving.

Wu took full advantage of the distraction and walked into the tower, knocking it down and sending blocks all over. He proceeded to laugh so hard that he looked like he might have an accident. Dad scooped him up and headed down the hall to get him changed. Mom followed.

Leich turned the laptop towards me.

— Mutts, look at this.

The Facebook page had exploded with activity, despite neither of us having spent much time updating it. We had more than a thousand people liking and sharing us on Facebook, and hundreds of wall posts and comments. He clicked on the Twitter tab, and the same thing was happening there, with well over a thousand followers and a busy #SecondChances hashtag. As I watched, five new followers appeared, the little red notifications button constantly updating.

— Holy crap, I said.

— And we had a record sales day yesterday. It had to be more than double our usual for a Saturday.

— Does Mom know?

— No, she'll find out Monday when she does the cash.

— Leich, you should have told her.

— It's hard to know how she'll take things these days.

— True, but this is good news, right?

He nodded but didn't reply, as the numbers on the red button grew. Normally, establishing a web presence took time and a ton of effort, but our social media sites seemed to be going viral for no reason at all. It has to be good, I thought, even as the sense of losing control rose along with the numbers.

— Are you two ready?

Leich and I had lost track of time. Mom had not. She eyed us up and down as we sat at the table, disapproval clouding her expression. But it was Sunday, I wanted to say. I didn't, however, get the chance, because Dad came back in with Wu, quite content with himself, having found matching outfits for the two of them that consisted of khaki cargo shorts and blue shirts.

— I wasn't sure what to wear to a church thing, he said.

— Can we stay home? I'm not sure I'm up for it, I said.

Leich agreed.

But that wasn't an option; Mom's will had a life of its own. Within ten minutes we found ourselves following her uncharacteristic spiritual desire towards Victoria Street and St. Paul's Church. Dad, Wu, Leich, and myself wore presentable but casual clothing, figuring that our neighbourhood wasn't going to fill a church with suits and skirts. Mom was more dressed up than the rest of us; she looked great, actually, and I even caught Dad sneaking a few appreciative glances.

We missed the service.

As we neared the stone church, we saw the head priest standing outside the front doors, shaking hands and speaking to his parishioners as they departed. We stood to the side as a large family trundled by, the mother and father looking harried as they shepherded four young children. The kids poked and prodded each other, released from an hour of hard wooden pews and impatient mother-pinches. More families came out, a mosaic of nationalities and ethnicities presenting themselves to God in their Sunday best. Suits and dresses, washed and pressed and bright. We felt terribly out of place.

The priest noticed us hesitating on the sidewalk and walked slowly over, leaving the handshaking to a junior clergyman. He was an older man in his seventies in wire-rimmed glasses and whom I'd never seen without a clerical collar. He visited the businesses in the neighbourhood about once a month, saying every time that he was just out for a constitutional and he thought he'd drop by. His white robe and the red stole harnessed across his shoulders were bright in the late morning sun, their formality contrasting with our clothing in a dramatic way. His smile was perfect, ministerial but non-threatening, his enthusiasm clear but restrained as he approached, hand extended.

— Gotta get the lost sheep back in the fold somehow, I whispered to Leich.

— Knock it off, Dad whispered.

The priest shook Mom and Dad's hands, and asked how they were doing in the aftermath of the robbery and the thief's surrender.

— We're fine, Father, thanks, she said.

Mom looked surprised to be asked, as though she had prepared herself for a healthy measure of priestly disappointment at our family missing mass. But it wasn't mentioned and they fell instead into a conversation about the store's new notoriety.

— Your store has become quite the focus of neighbourhood gossip, he said. I particularly enjoyed *The Spec*'s editorial about safety downtown—

— We were in the paper? I asked. Mom, did you know?

— A few people mentioned it at the last BIA meeting, she said. But I haven't read it.

— A few of my parishioners have stopped in, asking for prayers for you and the kids, the priest said.

— That's unbelievable, Leich said. Why would they care?

— Leich—

Mom gave him a glare, but the priest just laughed.

— People are funny, you know, he said. They might not give you a passing glance on the street, but everyone still watches everyone else. Does that surprise you?

— It does, actually, Leich said.

— Watch for it, the priest said. You'll see.

As the man talked about a few of the places in the neighbourhood that were generating buzz I began to feel embarrassed about my earlier sarcasm. His concern was genuine, his warmth deep, his smile broad and infectious. You should never begrudge the enthusiasm of someone who wants you to feel welcome, even if you're not sure how to receive it.

I excused myself—my discomfort made me want to avoid more small talk—and stepped onto St. Paul's manicured lawn, sliding off my flip-flops. The grass was cool. I dug into my pocket for my phone, again thinking about calling or texting Peter, but put it away without doing either. Instead, I walked towards the side of the church, looking up at the stonework and gothic windows. The cornerstone was carved with the date 1867. A small bronze plaque was affixed to the stone, inscribed with a long list of Irish-sounding names and benefactors.

I returned home on my own about thirty minutes later. Leich had received a phone call and disappeared while Mom and Dad were speaking with the priest. They'd accepted his offer to have lunch with him at the café the church ran at the corner of Wellington and King. Wu went with them, dead asleep in the stroller. I'd made my excuses and begged out of lunch; Mom hadn't argued, although she did give me a withering look. The alone time felt good.

There was a boy, perhaps ten or eleven, pressing his hands against the doors and trying to look into Second Chances. He was chubby and had on one of those silly ball caps with the shiny stickers and flat bills. He wore expensive basketball shoes so bright they could have glowed in the dark, long shiny shorts that rode low enough to reveal the brand of his underwear, and a sleeveless jersey that was way too large, making him look like he was excited about playing basketball three feet and ten sizes in the future.

— Store's closed, I said, unlocking the gate at the bottom of our stairs.

— That's stupid, everyone's open on Sundays now.

He was unaware of the contradiction between the shuttered storefronts and his words. If I had to stereotype him, I would have bet that he lived in the suburbs somewhere, in a huge house on a postage stamp lot, with an SUV perpetually idling in the driveway. He was too clean and soft to have come from downtown. He started pounding on the door's window, hard enough to worry about, yelling for someone to let him in. When he dropped the choicest of swear words and kicked the door, the better mood I had been in evaporated as quickly as a drop of water on a heated stovetop.

— Knock it off, I said in a raised voice.

— Who the hell are you?

— This is our store.

— Open up, then—I gotta get in there, he said, kicking the door again.

I pulled out my phone and threatened to call the police. He scoffed, looking at me with overfed arrogance, grabbed the door handle, and began shaking it. I tapped the screen and brought the phone to my ear, telling him the main police station was around the corner. With a final kick, he turned and ran off, heading right on Hughson and out of sight.

Brat, Suburban.

I imagined writing him into a story, where a blonde-streaked soccer mom waits for him around the corner in the family's second Escalade, ready to whisk him away to consolatory lattes at his favourite drive-thru. Her husband and his father had just left them for a younger woman, using words like forever and true love and just the way it is. Which made no sense, of course, because suburban soccer moms—grief-ridden or not—avoided downtown on principle, much less to bus spoiled sons through its streets and alleys as a form of therapy. But you can do that with stories, turn nonsense into reality.

— Hello? Hello?

Peter's tinny voice wafted from the speaker. I had hit redial rather than emergency call. I panicked and hung up on my best friend.

WEDNESDAY

I was awakened by the sound of laughter. Or so I thought—by the time I shrugged off enough haze to think about why I was awake when I'd been so deeply asleep seconds before, there was only the deadened sound of an apartment still at rest. It was hard to open my eyes—a layer of gunk had pasted my eyelids shut—but I felt great. For the first time since the dumping I'd slept through the night, dreamlessly as far as I could recall, in a kind of oblivion, and my stomach and heart hadn't constricted upon waking. I stretched, trying to squeeze every last drop of stiffness from my muscles, enjoying the feeling of the cool bedsheets beneath me and a freedom of breath I hadn't felt in days. Delicious.

I heard the laughing again. Maybe Leich or Dad had gotten up early to watch TV, I thought, stepping into some fresh jeans and pulling on a T-shirt. But when I walked down the hall, the kitchen and living room were empty. I was the first one awake. Then I heard it again, louder this time, without the dulled, echoic quality I'd heard in my room. It was coming from outside. Good-natured, the kind of early morning noise you heard at a street festival, where the performers and stall-keepers banter before the crowds arrive. I left the light off, went to the window, and looked down at our sidewalk. I had to rub my eyes to make sure I was seeing what I was seeing. There was a crowd of people in front of Second Chances, perhaps fifty strong, standing around in small groups, chatting, two-handing cups of coffee, and keeping an eye on the storefront.

I stared at them, not knowing what to do. Maybe I should wake everyone up, I thought. The clock on the microwave said seven-thirty, but it might as well have said noon—we'd never gotten up so late on a regular business day. A moment later, an exaggerated yawn announced Leich's arrival, partially answering my dilemma.

— Wow, it's quiet in here, he said. Did everyone sleep in?

— Leich, come here, I said. You have to—

— Not so loud, Mutts. I'm in the same room.

He stopped beside me, scratching his stomach, content as a sun-warmed dog, and squinted out the window. His eyes went wide. He was wide awake now, like me.

— How long have they been out there?

— I just woke up a few minutes ago too, I said, shrugging. It's seven-thirty.

— Really?

— Should we get Mom and Dad—

— Yes. No. Maybe—

He paused, considering, then nodded at the people.

— We can't open, he said. There's no way they'll fit in the store.

— We have to tell—

— Just wait. Let me think for a moment.

— Why? It's not our call. I'm getting Mom.

— Maybe we should let them sleep—

— Are you insane? If they decide to rob the place—

He winced, cutting me off, and brought his hand up to his temple where the scar pulled at the skin. Nice one, Mutton, I thought.

— Sorry, Leich. I'm an idiot.

— No, you're right. I'll get them—I can't believe they're still asleep.

I returned my attention to the crowd outside. A family of four arrived, the father's teeth bright against his beard, the mother's hijab a striking shade of indigo, the boy and girl assembled in identical outfits of yellow and pink. Three or four years old, I'd have guessed, although it was difficult to separate them by age. Twins, maybe, I thought as they giggled and tumbled around each other like hyperactive grapefruits. The waiting crowd welcomed them like old friends, the family blending into a clash of nationalities, colours, and classes, aligned by an invisible need to stand together in front of our store.

Our family, too, was just another shade on the abstract-impressionist canvas of the Hamilton downtown. There were pockets surrounding the city where communities clustered together, but our block and those surrounding us were so diverse they were almost undefined. No one talked about ethnic or cultural traditions much, preferring instead the universal languages of survival and trade. Concrete citizens. Urban loyalists.

Mom and Dad came into the kitchen in a rush of yawns and exclamations of surprise about the time, leaning against the counter over the sink to take in the crowd below, nudging me aside without realizing they'd done so. Leich followed them in and went to the fridge. He pulled out his breakfast things and began assembling them on the counter, his teenage-guy priorities re-established.

— There's so many, Mom said.

Dad wondered aloud if we should call the police.

— No, I don't think so, she replied. They're not making any trouble.

— They're even letting people through, I said.

As we watched, the assembly parted to let a man in a business suit pass. Despite the static limitations of the sidewalk, their movement was unexpectedly dynamic, like they'd become an entity, waving away and merging as smoothly as a kit of pigeons avoiding a church spire. A young couple dressed in black was next, their too-big clothing, studded belts, and chains swaying and glittering as they passed. Hypnotic.

— I'll help you and Leich open, Mom said. We'll just have to let them in one at a time.

— I thought Wu was meeting with that German specialist today, Dad said.

— Oh, shit, right, Mom said.

Wu shuffled in, groggy, his favourite blanket dusting the floor behind him. He beelined for Dad and hugged his leg. Dad scooped him up.

— Big doctor, Wu said. Oh, shit.

— That's right, little man, Dad said, leaning him towards the window to look at the people below. He's a big deal. But don't say that other word, okay?

— Big shit, Wu said.

Leich and I stifled a laugh. Dad let one out before he could stop himself, but Mom's expression cut him off, forcing an apologetic shrug. He put Wu down. As soon as his bare feet touched the floor, he went over to Leich and demanded breakfast. While Leich busied himself with Wu's juice and cereal, Mom turned to Dad and asked if he could possibly take the day off.

— The whole day?

— Well, the appointment is at eleven, but—

— You can never count on hospital time, Dad finished for her. I'm sorry, but I'm actually in court this afternoon, so I can't.

We all looked at him at the same instant, shocked.

— That's great news, I said.

— But you didn't say anything, Mom said.

— They're just small contract issues, Dad said. So it's not going to save our finances or anything.

— No, but every little bit helps.

Mom laid a light hand on his forearm and squeezed. She turned to me, telling me that we'd still open like usual and she'd call the specialist to reschedule. Dad and I protested— the doctor had flown in from Germany, after all—but Mom held firm, her eyes glittering with resolve. Dad held up his hands in surrender, glanced at the clock on the microwave, and said he needed to get ready. Then he backtracked and said he'd stay, that he could be a little late.

— No, go, Mom said. We'll be fine.

— Are you sure?

She shooed him down the hall and turned towards Leich and me.

— Okay, here's how it plays out, she said.

Her voice had changed, like she'd been asked to take over captainship of the losing squad in the game's final minutes and was psyching herself up for the job.

— Mutton, you and I will take turns with Wu. Leich, you're on door duty. We'll let them in only when people inside come out. No more than thirty in the store at a time, okay?

— Uh, sure, he said. Got it.

— They won't fit, I said.

— I think they will, she said. There's always more room than you think there will be.

— Leich, tell her about Saturday.

— What about it?

— The crowd, dummy. The record sales.

He smacked himself on the forehead.

— Shit, he said. Of course. I can't believe I forgot.

As Leich walked through Saturday's astonishing numbers, Mom took the story in without comment until the end, when Leich talked about how heavy the deposit bag was.

— So they were just there, waiting for you to open? Like today?

— Not so many, but it seemed like the store was full all day—never more than ten or fifteen, but—

— The space made it seem like more, Mom said.

— What could cause—

I stopped and pulled out my phone.

— Leich, check Twitter, I said, holding out the phone for him to see.

#SecondChances was going crazy. Every second the app would auto-refresh and a bunch of new tweets appeared, along with a torrent of comments and questions and excited planning. I flipped over to our Facebook page. There, the same story: people posting to the wall so quickly it could have caught fire. Mom looked confused, so we explained about the pages we had set up for the store, with me and Leich stumbling over each other's sentences to get the story out. Mom was briefly upset that we'd done this without her knowledge but proud at our initiative. And tense—how much did our publicity efforts have to do with the crowd outside?

— So what do we do about it? Shut the accounts down? she asked.

— I don't think so, Leich said. Thrift stores don't go viral. It must be something else.

— The Niche, maybe, I said.

— But it's just one thing, he said.

Yeah, but what a thing. We had stopped thinking about the Niche as anything other than part of the store's routine, something to watch, more products to sell. We took the Niche's magic for granted, that one person every day would be blessed by the little cubbyhole we had inherited. Still, we'd been seeing more and more people lately. The day before, when I came back to find that brat kicking the store's front door, I'd been distracted enough to ignore how unusual it was for him to be there on a Sunday. Mom asked a few questions about the publicity and social media, trying to get her head around what might be happening. Dad came back a few minutes later, tying his tie on the go. He asked some questions, too, standing beside Mom close enough that their shoulders touched. At the end Mom shook her head.

— No, the store's online presence might be a small part of this, but it has to be the Niche.

— But why now? Leich asked.

— Ever since the robbery—

I stopped, suddenly unable to find the words.

— The blond guy took the item, Leich said.

— And brought it back, Mom said, although that looked more like necessity than guilt.

— You're talking about this like the Niche has suddenly woken up or something, Dad said. Like the thief's mistake caused it.

— It sounds ridiculous to say it that way, Mom said. But—

— Not ridiculous, at the same time, Leich said.

We fell silent for a few moments, accompanied only by the strange soundtrack of the crowd on the street below. Wu, who looked unsatisfied with the quiet and serious expressions on everyone's faces, walked over to Leich and held up his hands. As Leich lifted and stood him on the counter, there was a sudden swell of laughter outside. Wu giggled along with the people below, looking at us to see if we were playing along, his eyes wide and delighted, like the crowd had gathered there just for him.

All day, the lineup outside the store didn't get any shorter. Leich and I took turns as gatekeeper, sitting on a stool and letting people in as those inside the store walked out. Mom stayed in the store with Wu almost all day, only leaving to feed him lunch and put him down for his afternoon nap. Since the stroke, he'd sleep for a couple of hours at least, much longer than before, forcing Mom to check in on him every so often just to make sure he was okay. It was hard to imagine such a tiny body needing such a volume of rest.

At five, an hour before closing, Mom brought Wu down. They squeezed between a middle-aged woman in red skinny jeans and a skeletal man with tattoos on every exposed patch of skin and joined me behind the register. Leich was on duty outside, undoubtedly scrutinizing his phone to keep from having to make small talk with the waiting customers. They wanted to chat, I'd also discovered, even though I usually had a novel in hand as my own shield. This crowd had a need to share confidential things, like family histories, arguments they'd had, secret hobbies they couldn't tell their families about. Odd.

— The specialist finally called back, Mom said. He'll see Wu tomorrow morning.

— I thought he was leaving.

— He said he was able to push his flight until the early afternoon.

— That's great news.

— I shouldn't be so surprised—people tend to go out of their way for Wu.

— You can't expect it, though.

— No, you can't.

She moved her eyes around the store, taking everyone in. Everything. Wu dug around the detritus under the counter, removing things one at a time. He counted the paper register and debit machine receipt rolls, pointing and reciting the numbers under his breath. We watched him pull out the sepia photograph and squint at the broken, starred glass, nodding at the picture as though he was satisfied that the glass, fractured though it was, still remained in place. When he slid it back into its spot, Mom and I exchanged a look with raised eyebrows, surprised that neither of us had taken the picture from him. Broken glass and cut fingers, after all. Accomplices in a brief moment of hazard. Finally, Wu reached into the lost and found box and rearranged a few things before pulling out a Transformers toy. He sat against the wall, manipulating the tiny robot's limbs, unsuccessfully trying to get it to turn back into whatever vehicle it was supposed to be. I knelt and offered to help, but he just shook his head slowly, never taking his eyes from the toy.

— Well, that's interesting, Mom said.

— I know, I said, standing. He's usually pretty good about—

— No, I meant about the bonsai tree.

She lifted her chin towards the Niche item, a tiny, gnarled pine tree in a rough ceramic pot we'd placed on a nearby shelf.

— There was a little girl looking at it earlier, I said. She was excited, and I just assumed she bought it.

Mom looked at the clock on the cash register screen.

— Has it ever lasted this long?

— Not while I've been in the store.

Mom leaned over the counter and yelled at Leich to come inside. He poked his head around the door, a dark silhouette against the golden afternoon sun outside.

— What's up?

— Tree's still here, I said.

— Huh. I thought the mini-tree girl bought it. Hey, Mutts, can you spell me? Seems like I've been out here forever.

I walked outside and sat on the still-warm barstool. The sidewalk was busy with people leaving their offices and heading back to homes and cars. The line for the store still ran the length of the building, reflected in Luigi's empty windows. The sheets of plywood in Razza's windows had been tagged, spray-painted squiggles revealing an occasional letter but mostly indecipherable. I'd often looked at the ubiquitous markings and wondered who'd done them, whether anyone other than the tagger could read them at all.

— Hey, can I go in now? Two people just left.

The man at the front of the line, a hipster in full beard, skinny chinos, and thick-rimmed glasses, was tapping his sneaker on the ground.

— Did they? I didn't see, I said.

— I've been waiting all day, you know, he said.

No, you haven't, I thought, but I smiled as best I could.

— Sure, go ahead, I said. Have fun.

— Better be worth it, he said.

As he walked past—close enough to force me to put my feet on the ground to keep from falling off the tall stool—a mutter of voices rippled back along the line, low and sullen, agreeing with the hipster. It was then that I noticed the lack of laughter, how different the people in the line were acting than those who'd appeared that morning. I apologized for the wait and explained that the store was just too small and that we'd do our best to get everyone in before closing at six. I tried to keep it light, but it felt forced. My words were passed along the line, person to person, making me think about that circle game where you whisper a sentence to the person to your right and it's barely recognizable by the time it comes back. There were some complaints, as though they'd expected we'd stay open until everyone got inside, and a few people near the end of the line threw up their arms and walked away.

When those at the front of the line saw them leave, they pressed even closer to me and the door, like they were afraid they'd be compelled by the urge to leave too. I was forced to hop from the stool, awkward and off balance, and the stool tipped over, the hardwood hitting cement sharp against the sounds of pedestrians and traffic.

— Mutton! Are you all right?

There was a light but steadying hand on my shoulder and a flash of earth tones in my peripheral vision. Peter had managed to sneak up without me noticing. He's ditched the crutches, I thought. Wait. Had the doctor given the okay?

— Mutton?

— Peter. Hi. Yes, I'm fine. Where did you—

— I wanted to come by and talk, he said. After you called the other day—

— I called?

— You didn't say anything, but I just assumed you wanted to speak with me. That's why I'm here.

I remembered hanging up on him instead of calling 911.

— Oh, that. Right.

— I've been texting but you didn't respond, so I thought—

I pulled out my phone, which I hadn't thought about since my last gatekeeper shift on the stool. A cascade of notifications tumbled down my screen when I turned it on.

— I'm sorry, I said. I didn't notice. All these people—

— No, I'm sorry, he said. About the other day. When you told me about...him.

— It's not your fault—I was the insensitive one.

A young couple walked out of the store, laughing, their arms full of second-hand things. The next people in line started to badger me to go in, but I held up my hands and told them to wait. I wanted to go back into the store and get a sense of how many people were there—for some reason, I couldn't remember how full it had been when I'd taken over from Leich. But Peter stood between me and the door.

— No, I'm your friend, he said. So I should have—

— Just a second, Peter. I have to go inside for a moment.

— It's just that—did he hurt you in any way?

— What? No. Well yes, I guess. He did break up with me by text, after all.

— That sucks.

— Thanks. I—

Another person walked out of the store, squinting against the brightness.

— There's another one, yelled an elderly man who stood a few people back from the front of the line. She's not going to let us in!

Almost as one, the line shuffled forward a step, pushing me closer to the door. More grumbling, growing in intensity, echoed against the windows and concrete.

— That's just so cowardly, Peter said. It makes me want to hurt him.

Agreed, I thought. But I didn't get to say anything. A small group of people walked out of the store, each carrying old shopping bags full of clothing. I felt the line tense, as though ready to pounce on me and the store, when an old woman in a grey pleated dress, easily in her eighties, walked out carrying the bonsai tree. The old man who'd spoken moments before uttered a strangled kind of howl and lunged for the old woman, knocking the tree to the sidewalk. She stood there, stunned, watching the man fall to his knees and scrabble around for bits of pottery and clumps of soil, muttering about the tree being his, her nerve at stealing it, and how long he'd waited. The line had stopped moving and everyone watched the man, transfixed. He leapt to his feet with surprising agility, tucked the whole mess under one arm, soil and pottery tumbling back to the sidewalk, and with the other dug a battered five-dollar-bill from his pocket. He wedged the damp money into the woman's hand, glaring at her with coke-oven intensity, and walked away, looking back over his shoulder as he went.

I stood beside the lady and looked her up and down. She began to shake, and a flush crept past the silver cross pendant at her clavicle, up the loose folds of her throat, and into the pale lines on her ancient face. She squinted after the man. I asked if she was all right.

— Bastard, she said.

She crammed the five-dollar bill into her purse. And spat. Hawked up a thick gob of anger, spat it to the concrete where it sat glinting like some hateful jewel, and stormed off after the man. I didn't know where to begin with my surprise—Her anger? Language? Spitting?—so I stood there, focused on the back of her diminishing but perfectly ironed dress. I heard Peter somewhere off to my side, saying something about still needing to talk. Then I heard the heavy sound of the store's front door closing, and the clunk of the locks. While Leich watched the door, Mom argued with a customer who'd come outside with them, a chubby, dark-skinned man in a stained track suit.

— No, she said, I'm not calling the police.

— But she punched me! And took the goddamned tree right out of my hands!

— She did pay you for it.

— That's not the point—I saw it first!

— There's nothing I can do about it.

The guy left, grumbling and cursing, thrusting his hands so deeply into his track suit pockets I thought he might tear right through them. Still feeling rather detached, I heard myself asking Leich what happened. His eyes were on the clumps of soil and shards of pottery on the ground.

— That guy and the old woman got into it over the Niche item, he said. They were the only customers left in the store. Mom and I were wondering if the line had finally been taken care of.

— No, I just didn't track the numbers enough, I said.

Mom moved to the edge of the sidewalk and cupped her hands around her mouth.

— I'm sorry, but Second Chances is closed for the day! We'll open again tomorrow!

With a swelling chorus of groans and disgruntled comments, the line dispersed quickly, taking the tension with it and leaving Leich, Mom, and me alone on the sidewalk. Oh, and Peter. Just as I started to tell the story of the old man stealing the bonsai from the old woman, he interrupted me by tapping me on the shoulder and asking again if we could talk. I tried to put him off, telling him to wait, but he was insistent. Which annoyed me, to be honest.

— Jesus, Peter, not now, I said.

— But—

— Are you—

I stopped myself, just in time, from using a word like stupid or dense. I closed my eyes and pinched my forehead between my thumb and index finger. Took a long, deep breath.

— Go home, I said. I can't deal with you right now.

I didn't tell him I'd call or reassure him that we'd have a chance to talk. I just dismissed him and turned back towards Mom and Leich to fill them in. I didn't see him leave, because the three of us were immediately absorbed by what had just transpired. The downward spiral of the crowd's mood as closing time drew near. The bizarre conflict around the Niche item. Three people had invested themselves in that tiny evergreen tree, but what occupied us the most was trying to figure out which of the three was supposed to have taken it home. In the end, we hoped that it was meant for the old man, as foul and mean-spirited as he was. We knew what had happened the last time the wrong person walked out of the store with that one perfect thing.

This time, there was no mistaking what woke me up: chanting filled my room. Leich, Mom, and Dad beat me to the kitchen, where the sound was impeded only by the double-paned windows over the sink. The microwave clock glowed 4:45 am. It was still dark outside, but every pool of streetlamp light was full of people. In the park, the bodies seemed to vanish in the dim darkness between the lamps, but on the sidewalk below hundreds of people moved, shoulder to shoulder, towards and away from our building and chanting.

— *OPEN UP!*

— *OPEN UP!*

— *OPEN UP!*

I reached for the light switch.

— No, don't, Leich said. Then they can see us.

It felt like all of Hamilton was down there, from construction drones in their reflector vests to senior citizens, caned and walkered. I wondered aloud why the crowd didn't simply storm the store—there'd be no stopping them.

— Yesterday's crowd could've done that, too, Leich said. But they waited for us to let them in.

— They've even left a little space around the doors, Mom said, leaning closer to the window.

Sure enough, there was a small semicircle of empty concrete just in front of Second Chances. The stoop was too far to the side to see from the window, but I had this sense that it, too, had been granted a small half moon of space.

— They must have been gathering all night, Dad said.

His voice was thin, strained. Leich must have heard it, too, because he grabbed the cordless and dialled 911, his hand shaking as he walked the dispatcher through what we were seeing. Whomever was on the other end of the line didn't believe him, because he had to repeat himself a few times.

— I don't know why no one else has called about it, he said. I know the police station is literally around the corner. Yes, I know how it must sound—

Dad reached for the handset but Leich waved him away.

— Finally! I mean, thank you. Please hurry, he said and hung up.

— They didn't believe you, I said.

— Would you?

— Well? Mom asked.

— She'll send someone over, Leich said.

My father asked how many cars they were sending, and when they would arrive.

— She didn't say, Leich said.

At the edges of the crowd, on the far side of Gore Park, more people were arriving. They took up the chant immediately. The chanting never let up, its synchronicity alarming and precise. When Leich slid open the window over the sink the chanting was a tide filling our apartment with an oceanic roar.

Eventually, we heard a siren. We watched a single police cruiser stop on King, its lights flashing. It barked out an alarm or two, but no one stopped chanting. No one even looked at it. The cruiser's doors opened, and two officers stepped out, eying the crowd but remaining within an arm's reach of the car. They fidgeted like schoolboys watching their first unfair fight, unable to pull themselves away from the fascinating reality of watching a good pummelling.

Mom growled a low curse and made for the door. Dad stepped in front of her.

— They're just standing there, she said.

— I'll handle it.

— It's my store.

— I hear what you're saying, but it's my building, Anne. Stay. Take care of the kids.

He walked out without waiting for an acknowledgment. To my amazement, Mom didn't object—normally, she would have let him know exactly how she felt about being told what to do—and let him go. She joined Leich and me at the window. We followed his progress towards the cruiser as the crowd moved back, like a single pond ripple skirting the water's edge. He walked straight for the car and began arguing with one of the two cops. The officer shook his head, his body language stating clearly that Dad wasn't getting anywhere. When Dad pointed towards us, the cop merely looked up and shrugged. The other officer pulled his radio handset from his vest, listened, and yelled something to his partner. Both men removed their caps and got back into the car. When the cruiser backed up and out of our line of sight, I really started to worry. Dad made his way back along the edge of the crowd, the ripple moving in reverse.

— He said there wasn't much to do if they weren't threatening anyone, Dad said when he came back into the kitchen.

— That's ridiculous, Mom said. They're blocking King Street.

— That's what I told him. But until they actually do
    something—
He trailed off, but we finished the thought in our minds.
There was little to be done.
— They looked afraid, Mom said. But still, wouldn't
    they call for backup?
No one responded, and we went back to looking at the
crowd. Our new silence against the chanting made me
realize how loudly we'd been talking. A soft, pre-dawn light
had begun to sift through the downtown, revealing the
extent of the crowd. In both directions, King Street and
Gore Park were full of people yet it seemed as though the
rest of the city slept on, unaware. It was unfathomable to
me that so many people could gather without attracting
notice. I went into my room and pulled up Facebook and
Twitter on my phone, but both sites were offline. Back in
the kitchen, I showed Leich. He started to blame our Inter-
net provider or the router, but dropped his objection when
he grabbed his phone too, also seeing the two sites down
but other pages loading without interference.
— That can't be because of us, though, he said. Right?
— I don't know, but I can't think of another reason, either.
We showed Mom and Dad, but they were too distracted
by the crowd to process unfamiliar news in the already
unfamiliar social media world. Online burdens being ours
to bear, as it were.
Mom looked back towards the darkened hallway.
— I can't believe Wu hasn't woken up yet, she said.
    He'd love this.
— I don't know, Dad said. Might be too much for him—
    that's an awful lot of people. Look at how freaked
    out we are.

— Lazy is all it is, Leich said.

Deadpan delivery. I suppressed a smile.

— Kid should face the day like normal people, I said.

— Can't sleep your responsibilities away, Leich said.

— Guys, knock it off, Dad said.

An almost-moment of release trickled away. When the cordless phone rang, its electronic chime insistent, we jumped. Dad grabbed it. After a moment, he covered the mouthpiece.

— It's 911 calling back, he said. The police, actually.

We waited while he finished the call, listening to his single-word responses and terse thank you at the end.

— The desk sergeant told us to sit tight, he said. They're getting their people together. I guess the crowd took them off guard, and since no one is being violent, they're working through a solution.

— A solution, Mom said, her voice flat.

Dad just shrugged and turned to the window again. Mom watched his back. I could tell what she was thinking, that she wanted to say something but didn't know how it would land. She was asking herself where the resolve he'd shown a few minutes before had gone. When he'd walked right out and through that crowd, like his confidence alone had caused the people to move aside. I was wondering the same thing.

The crowd stopped growing sometime between eight and nine. Realizing that the store wasn't going to open, they'd stopped chanting. In fact, everyone had finally turned away from the store and towards each other, as though discovering in the absence of sound that there were other people around. They huddled in small, chatty groups, occasionally looking at the store like it was a concert stage and they were just waiting for the main event.

The police response was a quiet one. They closed King Street at Catherine, diverting traffic north along King William and back to James. The flashers on the diverting cruisers strobed along the buildings and over the heads of the assembled crowd. A fire crew idled on Hughson Street. Patrol cops in yellow vests meandered around the edges of the crowd while a small army of riot police waited beside their bus on John Street, fidgeting with their gear and sharing cigarettes. An evacuation warning hadn't gone any further than that, the calming of the crowd having a parallel effect on the nerves of the authorities. Mr. Ahmad had parted the sea to set up his cart, and was doing a brisk trade in breakfast falafels.

I spent some time unsuccessfully writing about what was happening outside, trying to keep busy, feeling about as useful as the dirt on the windowsill. Taking advantage of the calmer atmosphere, Dad was working with the police down at street level and Leich had left to run what he called an urgent errand. He didn't notice the look Mom gave him as he waved a half-hearted goodbye, leaving her to get Wu—who'd slept in past eight—ready for the specialist's appointment. I tried to talk her out of going—Uh, Mom, I said, you do see the thousands of people outside, right?—but she could be so stubborn. Hard today, pliable tomorrow.

Mom had found some equilibrium, and under her worry and resolve there was also an eagerness to her movements. A hopeful anticipation. I understood. We knew how fortunate we were that Wu's specialized health care was so accessible, but even the stylized rituals of the progeria team were susceptible to the dulling effect of routine. So when the chance came around to learn from a new set of highly trained eyes and a top-of-the-field brain, you grabbed it. The German doctor had called us one day out of the blue, and I remember how excited she'd been when she got off the phone, how touched that he'd personally called to speak with her. So now, as she simultaneously tried to get dressed and remain in step with the dance of getting a three-year-old ready to leave the house, she had this glint in her eye that I really admired. It also reminded me how useless I felt, so I got up and packed some snacks and juice boxes into the stroller. Minutely more useful.

— We shouldn't be long, she said around a bobby pin in her mouth.

I shooed her away and finished dressing Wu myself. He was tired, probably from the early excitement, and let me do the work. In my haste, I accidentally pinched the folds of his wrinkled skin in his elastic waistband.

— Ouch, Mutton!

— Sorry, buddy, I said.

— You'll be all right? Mom asked.

— I'll be fine, I said.

— Right. Ready, Wu? The doctor is waiting, so this could be a big day for you.

He gave her a tired smile.

— Big day for me, he said.

I grabbed the stroller, she grabbed Wu, and I helped them down to the sidewalk, where the police had cleared a narrow path. As they walked towards the bus stop, Wu tried to wave at Dad, who was huddled with a couple of cops. Dad didn't see him, though.

Back in the apartment it was entirely too quiet. I opened my journal again and stared at the page. My phone sat on the coffee table, silent and dark. I picked it up and began going through my apps, one after the next, without really looking at them. I scrolled through my contacts, which went far too quickly. Peter's name, number, email, and photo were suddenly on the screen, and brief regret sung along my conscience. I hit the Call button.

— I'm sorry, the voicemail of the person you are trying to reach is full. This is a recording.

Well, of course it was a recording—did anyone still need to be told that the tinny voice wasn't a real live person? I sent a text apologizing for everything and asking to see him, but there was no way to tell if he received it or not. Texts didn't bounce back, but were just held indefinitely in cyberspace. That's how Peter must feel, I realized. Having shown me his feelings and having me just respond like everything was the same, leaving what he'd shared suspended in the ether. And then reaching out again with a peace offering, which I dismissed, knocking it to the ground and leaving it to rot.

Way to go, Mutton, way to go.

Rattled pounding on the street-level gates and repeated rings of the doorbell woke me from an accidental nap. I got up, squinting at the time on my phone, dizzy on my feet. Though I'd been out for only fifteen minutes or so, I was as disoriented as if I'd slept for hours.

I fell asleep, I thought. How the hell did *that* happen?

More pounding. And something else in the air, too. White noise, maybe, like the sound of forced air through ductwork you never actually notice because it's always on. The sound against the door grew heavier as I descended, the voice on the other side saying that it was the police and ordering me to open up. I swung the door back to reveal a huge police officer in black riot gear—seriously, he had to be seven feet tall—raising his fist for another round of gate rattling. And the noise, a roar of angry voices behind him.

— You have to leave, miss. Now, please.

— How did you know I was—?

— Your father told us. Is anyone else home?

I shook my head and opened the gate.

— Let's go, he said.

He shielded me from the roiling crowd with a large curved sheet of Plexiglass that pressed hard against my shoulder. A band of white stretched across the inside of the shield right next to my face, POLICE blocked off in black letters in reverse. I would not be exaggerating if I told you that it was like moving in his shadow. The rest of the riot police were no longer idling around their bus, but lined up purposefully to face the crowd.

The crowd was on its feet, every last person, yelling and surging towards the storefront. I saw a documentary once that had no narration or script, just short film clips strung together to create a narrative of raw images and sounds. In one of the scenes, filmed from overhead, a crowd of indigenous people was blessing the newest member of the tribe by surrounding him on all sides and chanting. As they—dozens of people—chanted, they moved towards and away from him in rhythm with their voices, rushing him and at the last second pulling back. What was most amazing was the crowd's unity and their synchronized movements. The rush towards the young man was frightening, the retreat like a full, relieved exhalation.

I didn't get it at all—if it was the Niche item that had drawn the crowd, why hadn't they stormed the store? I knew that the item was waiting in the little hole in the wall—if they really wanted it, there was no way the police would be able to stop them. The crowd seemed to pull and push against itself, anxious yet afraid, driven yet restrained. Not calming down.

I started looking at faces, blurred by their own jarring movement as well as my own stumbling behind the officer. There was a common focus, a need, to be right there in that place at that time. My eyes landed on a young girl in the heart of the crowd, four or five years old, dressed in a cream-coloured, billowy shift embroidered with flowers, her hair in a single knotted braid. She moved in tandem with the people around her. Like she was in a production, choreographed alongside an entranced, misfit cast of curbside players.

I stopped, the officer's gloved hand ripping away from my sleeve, and took a step in her direction. I have to speak with her, I thought.

— What the hell are you doing? the cop roared.

— She can tell me—

— Jesus, keep moving!

— No, I just—

He swore and grabbed me around the waist with his free hand, throwing me over his shoulder as though I was made of nothing. He's so pale, I thought, noticing the whiteness of his exposed skin under the lip of his helmet as we moved. Nerves and adrenaline. More human. He dropped me behind a barricade where Leich, Dad, and a few cops in regular uniforms watched the crowd. Dad was looking at his phone. Leich had his up to his ear and covered his other with his hand. After a moment, he shook his head and shrugged.

— What's going on? I yelled at my brother. When did you get back?

— We can't get a hold of Mom!

The park seemed like it had disappeared under the crush of people. A hungry, dissatisfied crowd is one of the world's great forces, unpredictable and alive. Even the reinforcements that had been called in, the riot police, extra patrol officers, EMTs, and standby fire crews, looked as nervous as we felt. Even in numbers, they looked small. Their concern was for the downtown and the safety of everyone else, taking the weight of the crisis so we could focus on the store and our home, full of our memories and things. Our lives.

I found myself again scanning faces, hoping to see Mom and Wu. After some time, I was horrified to realize that I'd begun to look for another face: between the undulating bodies and the flashes of clothing and movement, I watched for a careless flip of dark hair, a scruffy shoulder bag, black Chucks, and a hideous black and pink striped scarf. Forget about blood of my blood, I was worried about the guy who'd dumped me via text message, hoping to see his infuriating face come through. For him to be okay.

Me, Stupid.

Come on, Mutton, pull yourself together, I thought, turning my back on the crowd. Leich asked if I was all right. Dad chimed in as well. I waved them away, embarrassed, their concern like the pressure that builds after you gulp down too-hot coffee—you already know the liquid is too damn hot, and then you have to deal with the superheated, leaden ball inching its way down your esophagus, too.

If I hadn't looked away, though, I wouldn't have seen The Outfit standing at the edge of the crowd, shouting directions to his goons.

— Hey, look, I said, pointing. The Outfit!

— Who? Dad yelled.

— The Outfit! He's here—

Dad and Leich looked to where I was pointing, but it was like trying to direct their attention to a grey sweatshirt: invisible by every measure except to the person who saw it first.

— Nothing, I yelled. It's no one.

Three of The Outfit's men disappeared into the belly of the crowd, pulling bandanas over their faces and tugging the brims of their baseball caps down. It was amazing that I had seen him at all, as short as he was, how crazy the moment was. His goons were conspicuous, though, their covered faces and shifty eyes so different than the rest of the faces in the crowd, which were open and focused, almost in a trance. Maybe he's behind the crowd's appearance, I thought, before dismissing the thought. No, he and his men stood apart so thoroughly, their focus clear and distinct, as though they'd been handed an opportunity they couldn't refuse. But opportunity for what? Nothing good. I tried to yell at the cops, but they didn't seem to care that I was trying to get their attention. The decision had been made to move their command post farther down King, and we were being pushed towards the new location as the crowd roared.

The courts would never establish who threw the bricks, although we know it was one of The Outfit's men. The dark bubble eyes of the security cameras overlooking the intersection and park had been disabled. And although most of the people from the crowd would later apologize for their actions, leaving notes and letters in front of our door and posting dozens of messages online, to a person they would not remember anything, as though they'd been put under a spell. And the bricks, in that ubiquitous and dusty Hamilton orange, had been brought along for the occasion, having been made only weeks before at a foundry up the escarpment. Untraceable. Like fate.

We watched the first brick as it arced towards the store and shattered the glass of the display window. Two or three more bricks followed, smashing the neon OPEN sign and starring the safety glass of the door. The report would identify the source of the fire as sparks from the neon sign cascading down onto the vintage clothing below, smouldering for a few minutes before whispering into flame. But no one saw this, distracted by the surging mob, its tone shifted by the violence of the thrown bricks as quickly as a thought. We didn't see the smoke or the fire through the mass of bodies, but the roar of sound increased, and we held our breath, knowing the crowd was about to explode.

Dad paced behind the barricades that had been erected to keep pedestrians and onlookers from the crowd, furious about being kept away from the store and our home. He yelled at the cops to let us through and only quieted down when one of the beat cops started towards him, cuffs drawn. Leich and I, too, wanted to rush in and get upstairs, if only to lock our door and block out the unsafe world. The riot police had lined up and had started to advance towards the crowd, masks down, batons rattling against their plastic shields. We were close enough to see that they were amped up but nervous, as though all the training in the world couldn't quite prepare them for staring down unarmed citizens with the threat of violence behind their eyes.

Leich saw the smoke first.

— Fire!

Dad and I strained to see above the crowd. A wisp of smoke wafted up against the darkness near the top of the smashed display window, just visible from where we stood. Dad lost it, grabbing the nearest officer by a scruff of uniform material and spinning him towards the store, yelling at him, look, do something, move, move, move! The cop got angry, wrenching his clothing free from my father's grasp and snapping open an extendable baton from his belt. I panicked, stepping between him and my father, not caring about batons or guns or cuffs. It was a wonder that we weren't arrested right there, but just as the cop's eyes flashed red, he looked past me and saw the smoke too. He swore loudly enough to hear above the crowd and pushed over to his sergeant, gesticulating towards the storefront. But there was nothing to do. The crowd, having managed even to stall the riot police, was still too much in control to let the fire teams move in. The first flames licked the air above the crowd.

Then, a change. At first, it was a humming in the air, a breeze, maybe, the hint of sunshine behind thinning clouds. The sea of faces turned towards the intersection of Hughson and King.

— Dad, look!

Leich had climbed onto the pedestal of a nearby lamppost and was pointing over the crowd. Dad jumped up and balanced on one foot beside my brother, holding onto the post with one hand. For a long, frustrating moment— there was nothing else to stand on—I stood there, unable to see what they were seeing until I spotted SATAN'S FALAFEL in blazing yellow and red moving rapidly above the crowd towards the store like an apparition. And I heard Mr. Ahmad above the noise of the crowd, as furious as if his family honour were being challenged. It shouldn't have been possible for me to hear one voice right then, no matter how loud, but there it was. Remarkably, the crowd began to move away from the store, scattering in front of Mr. Ahmad, the Red Sea parting for Moses, as he pushed his cart in front of Second Chances. He snarled and punched the air, shouting for everyone to get back, stunning the crowd into silence as the flames began to fill the windows behind him. He roared. Every last person in that park that day heard it.

Even more improbably, I saw Peter move in from the far side of the crowd and leap through the flames in the display window. Where had he come from? How long had he been nearby? He ran so fast it seemed almost like a dream, but he was limping the entire way too. I gasped.

— Peter! No!

That was my futile effort to stop my best friend.

Mr. Ahmad leaned over and, releasing the bright red fire extinguisher strapped to his cart, proceeded to attack the flames, which were now billowing thick, black smoke. Everyone watched Mr. Ahmad battle the fire. Us. The crowd. The police. Maybe we were breathing.

The extinguisher sputtered out the last of its foam and there was a long beat of silence. One of the fire guys waiting by his rig swore and grabbed a large extinguisher from one of the truck's many compartments. He sprinted over and took over for Mr. Ahmad as his colleagues burst into action, stumbling over themselves to get to work. The crowd began to move with incredible efficiency, melting away from the park.

It was over within a few minutes. The police dragged back a couple of barricades and the firefighters drove in, ran a couple of hoses from the nearest hydrant, and extinguished the fire. The smoke belched black to grey then white. Peter was helped from the smoking store, soaked and coughing and carrying something under his arm, and set down on the step behind one of the ambulances. As an EMT fussed over him, I walked over, torn by every emotion you might expect after witnessing such a reckless act. As an oxygen mask was levered over his head and a blanket draped across his shoulders, he handed over my register copy of *A Boy of Good Breeding*, soaked through and filthy.

— What did you do that for? You could have—

I couldn't finish my accusation. He pulled the mask away to reveal a sooty grin. There was a small patch of skin that looked untouched by the grime, hazy and pale, and I realized that he had smudged model glue there, an unthinking attempt to scratch an itch or shoo a fly away. I was just about to reach out and peel it off when he spoke.

— I wanted to save your journal, he croaked.

Well, that did it. The image of my journal, safe in the living room, popped into my head. The memory of Peter— beige, beige Peter—jumping through fire, coughing and blind and doing so just because that damn little book meant something to me, knocked me back a step. And after I'd been so mean to him and he had still loved me enough to risk, well, everything. It all came up, and I began to cry and laugh and apologize and hug his wet, beige soul.

So I kissed him. You bet I did. We knocked teeth and lips because we were at different heights and off balance and just so young, and his mouth tasted like fire and smoke, and then so did mine.

Even the fire chief couldn't say when we'd be able to go into the store or apartment to assess the damages. Dad, Leich, and I found ourselves on one of the benches in the park, out of breath and still reeling. The fire trucks and most of the police vehicles had packed up and left. The smell of burning plastic and clothing lingered.

The EMTs had taken Peter to the hospital and I was working out when I could go to see him. Dad was on the phone, calling his insurance people and the bank and who knows who else. Leich tried calling Mom again but she wasn't answering. The police had retrieved the bricks from the foamy mess and taken statements from Leich, Dad, and me about what we had seen. They looked uncomfortable when I mentioned The Outfit; his involvement would complicate matters.

And the downtown slowly returned to its normal pace. King reopened, apart from one lane still blocked off for the fire marshal and police vehicles. If it weren't for the flashing emergency lights along our stretch of curb, it could be any other weekday. After opening Duster's up for the lunch crowd, Jenny stopped by our bench to offer her condolences about the store. The regular crew of Rascal drivers and shelter folks set up camp around the fountain as soon as the police cleared out. Mr. Ahmad had put his cart back in its customary spot and brought us a few falafel sandwiches, waving away our thanks, embarrassed by the attention. It was hard to believe it was still morning and that everything had happened across the span of only a few hours. It had seemed like so much longer.

— Leich, I said, pointing. Guess who.

The Outfit was sitting on a bench opposite us, blatantly staring. He was back in a suit and sporting a blood-red tie; he waved, an arrogant smile playing across his lips.

— You gotta be kidding, Leich said, anger flushing his cheeks.

Next to him, Dad ended the call he had been making and laid the phone on the bench between him and Leich.

— The insurance guy will be here in thirty—

He saw The Outfit. A strangled sound escaped from his throat and he leapt to his feet, taking an aggressive step towards the other bench. The Outfit scowled and got up, too. I was hoping my father, who had a few inches and a bunch of pounds on The Outfit, would grind him into the dirt. We weren't violent people, but nothing would have given me more pleasure than to see the grin wiped from his face.

Dad's phone rang, the melody echoing cheerfully and the vibrating alert buzzing enough that I could feel it on my end of the bench. Leich picked it up.

— Dad, you need to take this, he said.

But our father was still moving towards The Outfit.

— Dad! Leich yelled, getting to his feet and following with the still-ringing phone.

Dad stopped. Leich never yelled.

— It's the hospital, Leich said.

Dad took the phone.

— Anne, my God. You wouldn't believe what's happened—

He came back to sit on our bench.

— That's all right, I can grab your phone later, when—

We could hear the tinny sound of Mom's voice speaking rapidly, but couldn't make out the words. Dad gasped like he had been punched in the stomach and leaned forward. There were a few more breathless and brief exchanges before he ended the call, promising Mom that we would be there soon. Leich and I put our hands on his shaking shoulders and asked what was happening, trading panicked looks and feeling helpless, as he struggled to speak. It might have been the day, but that momentary pause between end of the call and the delivery of what ended up being the worst news ever seemed to last forever.

Finally, Dad choked back a sob and gathered us into his arms. He kissed us both on the tops of our heads—he hadn't done that since we were very young—and told us that Wu had suffered a massive stroke. He told us it was quick and that Wu would've felt no pain.

I believed him.

But we say those words to comfort the living—the dead can't tell us the truth, can they?

We took a taxi to the hospital, enduring the banal commentary of a cabbie who realized far too late that his passengers weren't in the mood to talk. Leich sat up front and stared out the window as we drove along King Street, watching passersby and students undertaking their normal activities. I sat with Dad in the back. He stared at his phone, as though willing it to deliver us from what would happen next. His eyes would fill with tears, threatening to spill over. The crying would come later, when he viewed his son's body, the joyous creation of his wife and family's forgiveness.

My mother and one of the doctors were waiting for us in the ICU, just past the frosted security doors. We had to sign in before they would take us in, and I remember thinking how awful it was that we couldn't get in to see Wu on our own, that we had to be escorted like visitors in a prison ward. The doctor was a tired young man in scrubs and a wrinkled lab coat who worked extra hard to keep his eyes from meeting ours. Mom's hair was dishevelled, her eyes rimmed in red. She reached for Dad, and they held each other a long time, whispering, while the doctor studied his clipboard. Finally, she gathered Leich and me in as well, and we spent an extended moment taking deep, hitching breaths, not knowing what to say.

— They've kept him in the room for us to see him, Mom said, pulling apart and wiping her eyes.

— Is he—?

I stopped, not knowing how to ask.

— He looks like he's sleeping, Mom said.

We followed the doctor deeper down the ICU hallway. He paused in front of a glassed-in room with drawn curtains and asked if we had any questions. We shook our heads. He said how sorry he was, but that they needed the space and asked if we could keep our visit as brief as possible. Leich bristled. He wiped his eyes.

— What would be an appropriate amount of time?

The doctor winced, told us to let the nursing station know when we were finished, and stepped softly away.

— No, really, how many minutes? Leich asked the doctor's retreating back.

Dad moved in front of my brother.

— Leich, are you ready to go in?

He nodded, and Mom opened the door.

With death, you expect certain things. If someone has had a long life they'll be old and grey. A cancer victim will be bald and thin. Someone who has experienced trauma might be barely recognizable under bandages and dressings. But Mom was right—Wu simply looked like he was sleeping. The staff had arranged his covers smoothly across his tiny chest, and his pale hands rested at his sides on top of the blue blanket. He shouldn't look so normal, I thought.

Leich moved to the bedside. When he laid his hand on Wu's, he pulled it back—he'd later tell me he hadn't antici-pated how cold Wu would be—and began to cry. Seeing his little brother unresponsive and feeling the heat leaving his wrinkled body dissolved any sense of teenage cool he possessed. I had never seen him cry like this before, and it was terrible. The rest of us lost it, too.

After a few minutes, Mom composed herself and explained what had happened. They had been a few minutes late for the appointment with the specialist, dashing through McMaster Hospital. Mom was stressed but Wu enjoyed the stroller ride, laughing at every crazy turn, chatting up a storm on the bus ride over. The specialist was excited and grateful to be working with Wu and had already scheduled a battery of tests and lab appointments. While waiting for one of the scans, Wu, squirmy, had gotten out of the stroller to stretch his legs, walking from chair to chair and patient to patient in the waiting room. In high spirits. Charming everyone. Then, as he walked back to Mom, he simply stopped in his tracks, tried to speak, and collapsed. Mom leaped from her seat, but even though it only took a second or two, he was gone by the time she knelt next to him. The doctors and nurses were unable to resuscitate him.

— I knew right away, but they still had to try, she said.

In the end, no one came to the room to kick us out, even though we stayed with Wu for a long time. None of us wanted to leave, and I remember feeling strongly that we should stay as long as we could, as though by remaining by his side we could be more a part of the passing. At one point Mom and Dad left Leich and me alone with him, I guess to help us say our goodbyes, but we spoke to each other instead. We kept starting stories about Wu, which usually involved him getting into trouble or infuriating one of us, always including at least one mention of his impish, joyful grin. We never finished a single story, though, breaking down when we tried to get past that smile and the Yay! that had often burst through it.

Eventually, though, we did leave. We tried to say something that resembled a goodbye, but everything we said seemed inadequate.

As we walked into the large atrium in the centre of the hospital, a space filled with light and warmth in an otherwise cold building, we paused for a moment so Dad could call a taxi. The atrium was a place we knew well; Wu's illness had brought us through this open area so many times that it had lost any sense of distinctiveness for us. It was just another hall to pass through to get to appointments and tests. Just another reminder of Wu's extraordinary existence, his rarest of disorders. I'm sure it was busy all the time, but that day it was teeming with more people than I could remember having seen there before.

When we stopped so Dad could make that call, everyone else stopped too. Every late and harried person, every patient and doctor, every worried parent and sibling paused right where they were and turned to face us. The whole place fell silent. Not just the voices and footsteps, but the background noises, the PA announcements, the distant clinking of mugs in the coffee shop, the hoarse sounds of the ductwork. I felt dizzy, like we'd been dropped into a sensory deprivation chamber. I opened my mouth to say something about it to my parents and brother, but they hadn't noticed. Dad spoke softly into his phone. Mom and Leich waited beside him quietly. Dad ended the call and said the taxi would be there in a minute or two and we moved outside to wait. The sliding doors whispered closed behind us, cutting off the motionless, silent lobby, and we were again surrounded by the uncountable sounds of a busy city in motion.

An hour or so before we left for the funeral home, a couple of police officers came by the hotel to tell us that the investigations had finished and the necessary clearances had been obtained. We could go back to the store and our apartment. This was good news. After three days of stepping all over each other in an impersonal hotel suite, we were exhausted, our nerves stretched thin.

Especially Mom and Dad. That they had managed to function over the previous few days was a small miracle. Wu's death had been an unimaginable blow and they'd still had to go through the legalities and bureaucratic nonsense that followed the riot and the fire, the statements and questions tossed to and fro from the police, the fire marshal, the insurance company. Leich and I had tried to help, but were probably more a hindrance than anything.

As luck would have it, the news was delivered by that same short cop, and we tensed up when we saw him. But he removed his uniform cap—his partner did the same—and apologized for the intrusion. He looked my parents in the eye and offered his condolences, wrestling with his words when he talked about how Wu had always brought a smile to his and his colleagues' faces. The other cop coughed and looked studiously away, and we all had a tough moment. The small officer replaced his cap.

— Right. Well, uh, just make sure to let us know if you
  need anything, he said.
— We will, Mom said. Thank you.

After the cops left, Dad closed the door and looked at
his watch.

— We should get moving. They'll be waiting for us at the
  funeral home.

A morning funeral had been one of the first decisions.
Three nights before, the shock of Wu's death as thick in the
air as the smell of smoke on our clothes, we'd sat around
the suite's tiny kitchen table and tried to figure out the best
time to say goodbye. We agreed that our family's private
farewells should happen early, well before the blur of the
funeral and graveside services. The afternoon would be left
open, and we'd decide then how best to fill it.

— How much time will we have with Wu before—before—
  Mom lost her words and stopped.
— Before the main event, Leich offered.

What a crass thing to say. There was a beat, a moment
that could have easily gone wrong, until Dad snickered.
Horrified, he covered his mouth with a fist, but it was
too late—the inappropriate response was out there and
running. Leich, panicky, watched everyone, clearly not
having thought through his words. Mom giggled. Then
me. Finally, Leich grinned and we laughed together, and
kept laughing until tears spilled down our faces. I bet the
noise spilled into the hotel hallway through the door, and
I briefly worried that someone might have heard. But not
for long—it felt good to laugh again without worrying
about whether or not it was appropriate.

The funeral director met us at the front door. Overnight, a handful of well-wishers had deposited letters and bouquets of flowers in front of the doors, and he swept them up, telling us they would be added to the others that had been pouring in. The public visitations had taken place across the span of two long nights. Because of the rarity of his condition, Wu's death had made news all over the city and beyond, and we'd expected that there would be a lot of people. However, I don't think we anticipated just how many, and the torrent streaming through the largest parlour in the funeral home had lasted long after the staff drove our weary family back to the hotel.

— We've set up an extra parlour for the flowers and cards, the funeral director said.

— A whole room? Mom asked.

— They've been coming in since Monday, actually, but not to worry, we're keeping a log so you'll know who sent what.

We were led to the parlour where Wu rested in his tiny casket—so much smaller than I imagined it would be— and the director let us know we could have as much time as we needed. We walked in as a family, and stood in front of the open casket arm in arm, each of us lost in our own thoughts. Leich told a story about Wu melting one of his old trophies by leaving it wedged between the radiator and the wall. I remembered the first time he added Yay! to his greetings, and how he'd use it to get out of trouble when he misbehaved. Dad and Mom just listened and laughed along with our stories, enjoying that Leich and I were leading this family moment.

We moved into the hall after a while. Mom said that if we wanted to, we could have some time alone with Wu.

— Mutts, you go first, Leich said.

— No, you should—

— I'm not quite ready, sis. Can you?

— I can, if that's all right.

— Sure is, Dad said.

— Absolutely, Mom said.

I closed the door behind me and moved slowly across the room. The same space felt so different when I was alone, so much bigger, emptier. I stood again beside Wu's coffin. It was made of a dark wood with a matte varnish, the lining a cream silk that framed his head and upper body. Its polish and pristine interior made him look even smaller. As did his clothing, the creases in his dress shirt and trousers tenting the fabric away from his body. Diminished. How strange it was to bury Wu in a claustrophobic, alien space, dressed in rigid clothing he never wore in life. My baby brother's disease kept him small even as other boys his age grew big and strong, but here the casket and clothing made him look too much like he had given up too soon.

I tried saying some final things to him, but every word seemed forced, like I should say them rather than wanting to. Eventually, I stopped trying, and instead let my memories carry me. My eyes, already tired and raw from the previous days, filled again as I recalled how much life he had brought into our home, how he'd defied the limitations placed on him by his disease. How alive he'd been!

The one thing the undertakers hadn't gotten right was his wrinkles. With best intentions, they'd tried to smooth the folds and wrinkles from his face, so he looked almost normal and vibrant. But he looked wrong, too, like those flaws hadn't defined him enough to remain after he died. I reached over and tried to undo the top button of his shirt, hoping that perhaps releasing the button would relax his skin and restore the character I remembered. But his lifeless skin didn't relax, and opening the shirt just revealed the dead, transparent pallor of his throat. Tears streaming down my face, I re-buttoned the shirt, but my vision was so blurred that I ended up pinching Wu's skin between the folds of the shirt.

Ouch, Mutton!

Wu's last words to me.

I came apart. I fell to my knees, my hands covering my face, and poured out my furious grief to the too-quiet air. The last thing I had done was hurt my perfect baby brother and I worried that even in death he'd somehow know that I had. I wanted someone to comfort me, to say that of course Wu would carry only the good with him past the grave. Of course he loved me and would always smile and squirm when he saw me. Of course I would always be his favourite play partner. But no one came. In the stillness of that carpeted, curtained parlour, I couldn't make a sound, as though the cruel universe had decided to take my voice away, too.

Baby brother, baby brother, why'd you leave?

After the intimacy of my final, quiet moments with Wu, the funeral service felt like a circus. St. Paul's was packed beyond capacity, with mourners and well-wishers lining the walls and spilling onto the manicured lawn. We stepped out of the dark funeral home vehicles, entered the church through its huge wooden doors, and slid into the reserved front pew. Everyone we knew had come, from Peter in the second row to The Outfit and his muzzled goons at the back. The silence was pierced only by an occasional cough or creak from the worn wooden pews. Within moments, though, the focus shifted back to Wu's closed coffin at the front. We watched it, too—the boxes children are buried in create their own unavoidable gravity.

The head priest, in a swirl of vestments, stepped out from his office near the front of the church and took the pulpit. No procession, no bells, no cloud of incense to mark his arrival. Though he looked infinitely more formal than the man in the simple clerical collar who'd lunched with Mom and Dad, in deference to their preference for simplicity he wore only a robe and an understated stole. They'd insisted on a simple service, even refusing the services of the parish organist, preferring quiet contemplation to adornment or song. The homily was brief. The priest looked out over the assembly and admitted that he didn't know Wu nearly as well as he knew how people had responded to his death. He was not surprised by the turnout, how people had come from every corner of downtown and from every situation, from the rich and comfortable to the patched-together and destitute. He said that survival was about sharing in the daily rising and stumbling so necessary to move life forward. And to mark its end.

Stumbling indeed. Even back then, I knew so many good people always on the verge of losing their footing. Fallen, imperfect, sidewalk saints. I knew that they, that I, stumbled, but as long as there were sturdy things to lean against or strong hands to help us up, stumbling was never the final story. We looked for those solid places, those familiar, helping hands. To be known is a kind of survival, isn't it?

After the priest's remarks, Dad and Mom stood together and thanked everyone for coming, saying how much the city's support meant to our family. Moved but composed, betrayed only by the whiteness of the knuckles on their intertwined hands. I focused on the picture of Wu Mom had chosen to display at the front, taken on a brisk spring day when I'd managed to get Wu to stand still for a few moments next to those eastward-facing cannons. Who could have imagined that photo would allow him to look over his own funeral, with eyes as bright as the sky and his cheeks nipped with delicious pink cheer?

Dad, Mom, Leich, and I carried Wu. We shouldered the casket to the hearse waiting in front of the church, the weight appropriately heavy. At the graveyard, as we walked across the grass to the turf-lined hole in the ground, I tried to find a lightness in the burden, as though I might be able to leave some of my grief in the box we were burying my brother in. We laid the coffin on the nylon straps that would lower it into the hole and took our places.

The graveside service was just for family. The priest had made the suggestion when my parents had been at their most overwhelmed, and it was a good one. I wasn't the only one who'd spent a difficult few minutes alone with Wu, and we needed some time to come together and say a more final goodbye.

The sun snuck behind a thick, greasy cloud, filling the graveyard with a subdued, uniform light. Such a weird ritual, I thought, waiting for someone else to give a proper send-off to our loved one's remains. Leich and I respected Mom and Dad's need for simplicity and privacy, but we also knew that the day couldn't be big enough—in many ways, Wu deserved the biggest of everything. The day before, Leich and I had talked about funerals in other countries, where everyone turned out in big, singing crowds and the casket was passed from person to person, high above, until everyone had a chance to touch it. Here, there were only five of us, staring at a box suspended over a hole in the ground.

The priest's Bible remained closed, clasped under his arm, throughout the graveside liturgy. He'd memorized it, delivering the standard passages and sentiment. However, after casting holy water on the casket, air-signing the cross, and saying his amen, he didn't dismiss us.

— You loved him, he said.

It was at once a statement and a question. We nodded.

— You loved him fiercely and completely, and what you're feeling right now is a hole in that love. Faith can give you comfort—and I pray that it does—but the pain you feel right now, that fierce and complete pain, is also right and just. Good, even. The death of a three-year-old is supposed to hurt.

We exchanged glances. This was comfort?

— Still, he continued, you're going to have a thousand people telling you to feel better, that it gets better. You will, and it does. But right now, for my part, I sincerely hope that your family finds the space to grieve properly and well.

I found myself nodding again as his words opened me back up. Perhaps I had felt healing in the few moments it took to bear Wu to his resting place, perhaps not, but the priest was right: no matter how much healing took place, we would always feel Wu's loss. Always. In the coming hours and days, we'd hear innumerable variations of I Hope You Feel Better Soon, but as strange as it sounds, the greatest comfort I felt was in just feeling the loss.

The sun reappeared as the priest stepped to the side to let us approach the grave. Each of us had brought something of Wu's along, and we took turns placing our memories on the casket. Mom had chosen a faded and threadbare blanket that Wu had retired a few months before. Leich straightened the bill of a beloved stuffed monkey's jaunty red cap. Dad had dug into Wu's Duplo and fashioned a small house, complete with a window that opened to the outside and an in-swinging door. I chose a racing car in brilliant red, the paint chipped and worn at the corners. I had to lay it on its side to keep it from speeding away on its own, down the slick wood and into the darkness below.

Then we buried my baby brother. Some more good things were said, more tears were wiped away, and we squinted against the sun, which was as bright as I imagined it was on the day Wu was born.

We woke up to a pure-blue, perfect day. The drenching thunderstorms that had been predicted to lash Hamilton all night had never materialized. The streets were dry and no traffic-scattered puddles remained as evidence of an overnight deluge. I had slept well, the weight of the previous few days and the release of saying that final goodbye leaving me with little other than the need for rest. That morning arrived with a little more shine than many of the previous ones had, lightening the shadows under everyone's eyes. I was glad; we needed the sleep, and we needed the light.

We ate our breakfast in the hotel suite's small kitchen, standing around the cramped space and saying little, readying ourselves for the cleanup of Second Chances. And Wu. I knew we were still thinking about him, too.

Eventually—no one seemed to be in too much of a hurry to see what state our spaces were in—we exited the hotel. As we walked west along King, the traffic's wind was cool enough to raise goosebumps on my exposed arms. Leich walked beside me quietly, his phone out, tapping madly on his screen. A few paces in front of us, Dad and Mom held hands and spoke in low voices. Crossing James Street, we walked against the stream of businesspeople heading into work from the cheap spots east of downtown.

A police cruiser was parked unobtrusively down King a ways, the silhouetted officer inside raising a hand in greeting when we stopped in front of the store. Red and Blue, the twins, were sleeping in front of the store again and woke up as Dad tore down some of the police tape sealing the front door. There were still shards of glass and unidentified bits of charred material around the damp pieces of cardboard they were lying on. Mom, Leich, and I looked at each other and shrugged as, bleary eyed and stiff, they yawned and stretched their thin, dirty limbs. But what could we say, really? They stood and smiled shyly at us, fleeting sparks against the morning shadows.

— No one came into the store, Blue said.

— We made sure, Red agreed.

— You slept here all night?

They exchanged glances at Mom's shocked question.

— Every night since the baby died, they said together.

These two kids, whose lives had probably thrown more at them by this tender age than we'd ever know, had given us everything they could. And again, the police—who had promised to watch the store—had let them. Mom, Dad, and Leich went into the store as much to escape their emotions as to get started on the day's tasks. I thanked the two girls with a thick tongue, barely getting out the words. They fidgeted, embarrassed.

— Your brother was a nice boy.

Red said this in the matter-of-fact tone best delivered by the young, her sister nodding, as though that was enough explanation. Maybe it was. They knelt, gathered the damp cardboard under their arms, and walked away, disappearing around the corner at Hughson Street.

A couple of hours later, we stepped out from the store's gloom into the sidewalk's brightness and wandered across the street. It was time for a break. It had taken us that long to get our heads around how much there was to do. Three days without any ventilation had turned the sodden, foamy mess into a musty quagmire. Most of the store hadn't been doused by the enthusiastic firemen, but there was plenty of smoke damage and a swampy smell from the inventory that had taken the brunt of the attack against the flames. Thankfully, Peter's estimations of everything being wet had turned out to be a bit of hyperbole, an understandable exaggeration in the face of his well-intentioned efforts to save my journal. Leich ran over to Tim Hortons at the corner for some coffee and snacks and met us in the park, where Mom and Dad sat wearily on a bench and I had collapsed onto the nearby grass.

We had gotten as far as a system of division for the goods, breaking them down into degrees of damage that ranged from ruined to salvageable. Everything had been affected by the smoke, however. The oily, noxious fumes had seeped into every piece of clothing and a layer of soot coated most items, heavily near the front, less so near the back. It was as though every item of my mother's inventory bore evidence of the tragedy, either within or without. Dad had reported that the apartment was in good shape but smoky, and that it would be impossible to return until it had been cleaned. It was better news than we had feared, yet not as good as we'd hoped for.

— How much can we save? Leich asked Mom.
— Not much, I'm afraid. Smoke damage can be hard to
    sneak past inspectors.
— We can all clean, I said.
 She smiled.
— It might not be enough, Mutton, but thanks.

A dark car stopped in front of the store. No sooner had the brake lights flashed off when the police cruiser accelerated and closed the distance, lights flashing, belching a warning blast from the siren. The Shirt stepped out and gave the officer a wave, walked around to the passenger side, and opened the door, helping a young man onto the sidewalk. Saul. He kept his eyes on the concrete, rocking slightly and clutching his space pen. They stood together on the busy stretch of sidewalk looking at the front of the store as Rascals and citizens flowed around, stones in a swift current. In an instant we had gathered our cups and wrappers, and sprinted across King Street through a gap in the traffic. The police cruiser reversed to its former position and switched off its lights.

— What do you want? my father asked.

Neither responded. The Shirt's eyes scanned the store with a detached look and Saul rocked, rhythmic and silent, like always. After a long moment, The Shirt—out of uniform in jeans—turned towards my parents and greeted them by name. He extended his hand to my father.

— I'm sorry about your son, he said.

My father took the hand and shook it, as did my mother, Leich, and I.

— And I'm sorry we missed the service yesterday.

We were long accustomed to his tendency to politicize everything—he was a man on a mission, hoping to revitalize our downtown with cards and slot machines rather than culture and depth. Yet he appeared genuine. It was disarming, as were his red eyes and drawn features. Mom and Dad traded a quick look—I don't think any of us even noticed The Shirt's absence—and told him not to worry about it.

— I couldn't face it, The Shirt said.

He looked down at Saul.

— And then I made the mistake of telling my son we weren't going to the funeral.

— Saul's your son? I asked.

He nodded and explained that he had been given guardianship just a week earlier, when his ex-wife had passed away. There was a long story there, one I would learn in full much later, that involved hiding the pregnancy for political expediency and The Shirt being left for another man while Saul was still in the womb. The Shirt was now learning to be a parent and was completely overwhelmed and horrified by how Saul had been treated in the group home.

— I'm learning that when Saul says he wants something, he—

— But Saul can't talk, I said.

The Shirt tilted his head, confusion pinching his features, so Mom explained about Saul's escapes from the group home and how he'd come to our store, trying to soften the parts about the police and the abusive behaviour of the group home staff. He asked some questions about Saul's visits and Leich volunteered the story about Saul standing up to The Outfit and his goons, which made The Shirt smile.

— Well, today he fought to come here.

The trilling of Leich's phone interrupted the moment, its foreign sound a reminder that there was a bigger world beyond ourselves. Leich walked off to take the call in private. Dad asked The Shirt if he would like to come in and see the store for himself. He agreed, his face taking on its more public character, and we moved into Second Chances. The emergency lights Dad had arranged for the cleanup cast their harsh glare over the store's interior, creating dramatic shadows on the walls. The Shirt wandered around with my parents, taking in the damage, while Saul trailed behind. I stayed near the front, digging behind the register to see what could be salvaged.

Leich leaned in a few minutes later and said that he was heading out for a while, and was gone before Mom and Dad could react or ask when he would return.

— Now? I asked the closing door. Really?

— That's not like him, Dad said. Maybe I should—

— No, stay, Mom said. There's so much to do—he'll be back.

The Shirt thought for a moment.

— Could you use an extra pair of hands? he asked.

— Two pairs, Dad.

Saul spoke softly but clearly and returned to his silent rocking, turning the space pen in his hand with a busy thumb. Mom and Dad gratefully accepted The Shirt's offer. As it turns out, that would be the only time I ever heard Saul speak. Isn't it remarkable how our assumptions can blind us, obscuring the magic we haven't yet discovered? I like to think that Saul trusted us enough to say the right thing, and chose to keep the rest of his words for his new home and a father who'd been given a second chance.

We ordered pizza for lunch and set up some folding chairs— they'd been buried deep in a closet upstairs, escaping the smoky smell that permeated almost everything else—in front of the store. We enjoyed the fresh air and sunshine, the day having lost not a bit of perfection from its grand beginnings. It was the perfect temperature, just warm enough to sit comfortably, but cool enough that the sun didn't bathe us in sweat. The wind brought fresh, green air through the downtown. Between bites, The Shirt wondered aloud if it was the Niagara vineyards we were smelling.

— We should be smelling the mills, Mom said.

— I can't remember the last time we had an easterly that didn't smell like steel, Dad said.

Saul smiled a little as he rocked on his seat, like he knew exactly why the steel mills' ubiquitous exhaust was kept from the core.

— If only every day was this fresh, The Shirt said. But progress, you know—

His eyes brightened at the mention of the word progress and he sat straighter for an instant, looking as though he was ready to stump for votes. But then he chuckled softly.

— No politics today, he said.

— Thank God, Mom and Dad said together.

The three adults laughed and began drifting through topics like weather and local restaurants. The conversation had a surreal quality to it, like I was watching animals from different levels of the food chain finding themselves at the same watering hole. I got up and made an excuse about using the bathroom, but in truth I was having a moment of grief, uncomfortable with idle talk and pleasantries. At the back, the safe had been emptied and left open, its heavy door resting against its form-fit hole in the crumbling drywall. The Niche, though, was closed. I swung open the wooden door to find a small carving made of reddish wood, perhaps six inches tall, in the shape of a fiddlehead. Gorgeous, of course.

— What's that? Mom asked when I emerged into the sunshine.

— Niche item, I said. Must've been there since the day of the riot—

The day Wu died, I thought. I felt a flare of heat in my stomach.

— Niche item? What's that?

The Shirt had lifted his face towards the sun, half-eaten slice of pizza in one hand, looking drowsy. He didn't open his eyes.

— Just a carving I found in the store, I said. There's a small cubbyhole at the back—

I stopped, not knowing what to say next. It wasn't much of an explanation, but I had to say something. I hadn't thought about the Niche in days. Saul got up and held out his hand, surprising me enough to hand over the carving without another word. He moved beside his father, nudged him in the shoulder, and dropped it into his lap. The Shirt's eyes widened.

— Oh, my God, he said. This is kauri wood.

Before any of us could ask what kauri wood was, The Shirt dropped the pizza slice into the box and picked up the carving. He turned it over a few times, rubbing his fingers along its whorls and curves, describing how the Maori in New Zealand carve fiddleheads as symbols of new life and birth. His voice seemed detached.

— I collect rare woods, he said. This kauri could be more than fifty thousand years old.

He got up from his chair and turned towards the store. His eyes changed as he studied the length of the Weston Arcade. City Bingo's gaudy blinking lights tried somewhat successfully to compete with the sun. Razza's and Luigi's storefronts were dark but their signs were radiant; they could have been painted the day before. Carving in hand, The Shirt walked along the arcade's entire length and back, taking in every cornice and ledge of its facade. He dug a five-dollar bill from his wallet and handed it to me, sat, and grabbed his half-finished slice, unaware that we were openly staring at him. I hadn't quoted a price for the fiddle-head, nor had I even thought about charging him for it.

— It's a beautiful building, really, he said.

Mom and Dad exchanged glances wondering, no doubt, as was I, at the change in The Shirt's demeanour. He'd always been so aloof and dismissive of heritage and preservation in the city core, but here he was, seeing our building with new eyes.

— So many nice buildings, he said. Good spaces, you know?

— I couldn't agree more! Such excellent opportunity for development!

A familiar voice—The Outfit and his two gorillas had turned onto King from Hughson and stopped in front of us. He clucked his tongue and shook his head as he surveyed the sheets of rough construction plywood where the windows used to be.

— Anne, I am so sorry for your loss, he said. For your entire family's loss, to be sure.

— I think you should leave, she said.

— Such a tragedy, but I wonder how such things can be avoided in the future. I'm sure the city councillor will have some ideas—he's very practical about such things. Right, Councillor?

The Shirt said nothing, still chewing his pizza, lost in thought. Saul moaned and rocked more violently the more The Outfit spoke. The Outfit nodded at one of his men.

— You. Shut him up, please.

The goon took one step towards Saul, glancing back at his boss as if to make sure the order was serious. This finally broke The Shirt from his reverie, and he was up and in the goon's face in an instant, spitting out low words that somehow stopped the bigger man in his tracks. The Shirt seemed to double in size, ready to tear The Outfit's goon apart to protect Saul. The bodyguard took a step back, undoubtedly aware of the implications of manhandling a city councilman and his intellectually challenged son. The Shirt pointed at The Outfit with the fiddlehead and told him that he would no longer tolerate any threats to our family or to our building.

— Or any building, for that matter, he said.

The Outfit, surprised, shook his head.

— I am not sure where this is coming from, but it would be a mistake—

— I don't think so, The Shirt said. You'll need to find a new friend at city hall.

The Outfit's face grew red, a sharp contrast to his grey summer suit. His calm veneer dissolved, and he began to sputter a response, flustered and indistinct. He looked ugly, I thought, and far too human. The Shirt must have had a similar impression because he laughed out loud, further infuriating the diminutive mobster, who stepped forward and pushed The Shirt. His two men shifted on their feet but did nothing—aggression from The Outfit was unfamiliar territory.

Things might have deteriorated even further if Mr. Ahmad hadn't walked over in his white apron, stainless steel tongs in his hand. He stood beside The Shirt and faced The Outfit and his two neckless thugs.

— Hello, he said. May I make help for you?

His voice was perfectly calm, his posture as straight and rigid as if his spine was made of iron. I was reminded

224

of the day I saw him stand fast in front of the same three men. I remembered how quickly they blinked first and how mysterious Mr. Ahmad's defiance had seemed. Some of that mystery dissolved when, from my place a couple paces away, I saw the strength in his bearing, the muscles and tendons on his arms and throat clearly defined, how unafraid he was. In such moments you glimpse former lives—The Outfit's criminal life defining his methods, and the unknown, hard events in Mr. Ahmad's past strengthening him for those future times he needed to push back. For himself and for his loved ones. Like us.

I could see The Outfit searching for the perfect threat. But in the end, he simply sniffed, adjusted his tie, spun on a heel, and walked away. His men shuffled after him, confused, falling into position as unevenly as dogs getting used to their leads again.

Mr. Ahmad's face was kind when he asked if we were okay. We each nodded, still stunned by what had just happened. To my parents, he leaned in and offered his condolences, his voice trembling when he spoke Wu's name.

— Thank you, my mother said, blinking back her own tears.

His eyes full—again—my father didn't speak. He just reached out his hand, which Mr. Ahmad grasped with both of his own. Mr. Ahmad went back to Satan's Falafel in the park, giving The Shirt a quick nod.

— We have to save this building, The Shirt said, the carving held tightly in his hand.

It was a difficult day, despite the hopeful distractions and solidarity shown by our neighbours. Making our way through the ruined merchandise in Mom's store was a sobering task, made worse by the growing pile of garbage bags full of things we could never sell. She had been right about many of the items, whose ingrained fire-and-smoke damage would have required too much work to clean. All of the clothing was ruined.

I distracted myself by trying to reach out to Mom whenever I could, knowing all that wasted revenue had to be eating at her. And I know that the unexpected happenings, as dramatic as they were, might seem to have been effective diversions from our grieving, but there were long stretches of heaviness where no one spoke. Wu was never far from our thoughts—that day, perhaps more than anytime else, was the first day of the rest of our family's life without him.

Saul and The Shirt were sensitive to this. The Shirt immersed himself in the work, emerging at the end of the day as filthy as any of us but at peace, too—when he'd thought that no one was looking, he'd take the fiddlehead from his pocket and sneak glances at it. I found an old pair of Mom's iPod headphones under the cash register for Saul, and plugged him into my phone so he could listen to music. Leich had not returned nor had he been answering texts or calls, much to my parents' surprise and displeasure.

Sometime late in the afternoon, as we realized that we were running out of things to sort and bag, we heard the hiss and squeal of heavy brakes outside the front door. A moment later, Mrs. Nyman walked slowly into Second Chances, leaning on a cane. She saw me right away.

— Hello, young lady.

— Mrs. Nyman, can I get you a chair—

She laughed.

— Assumed an old woman can't walk, did you?

— No, I meant—

— I'm kidding, Mutton. It's good for me to stand. I use
that motorized thing too much anyhow.

Mom and Dad stopped their work and came to the front.
I introduced Mrs. Nyman to my parents, explaining that
sometimes she came around the store to browse, a small fib
she didn't correct. She offered her condolences.

— I had a son once too, she said.

No one tried to fill her pause for a long moment, until
Mom asked what brought her by. Mrs. Nyman explained
that the riot and the fire had been big news around the
downtown, so she thought that perhaps there might be
ruined goods we were thinking of throwing away. Mom
told her that everything was smoke-damaged and musty,
but Mrs. Nyman shook her head and gently interrupted.

— You can save just about anything, she said.

Mom took a second before responding.

— Of course—whatever you can carry, you can have.

— Anne, there's so much damage—

Mom cut off Dad's objection with a look.

— We'll just throw most of it away anyhow, she
said. This way we know it's getting another chance. If
one thing makes it into the right hands, I'll be happy.

Mrs. Nyman turned partway to the door, put her index
finger and thumb in her mouth and whistled. In seconds,
a guy with dark hair and a heavily tattooed neck came
in, leading three boys a couple of years younger than me.
When Saul frowned at the guy and turned away, I remembered: he was the belligerent group home manager who
had abused Saul right there in the store. But around Mrs.
Nyman, he was clearly under orders to do as she wanted.

I think we must have looked shocked by her impressive
whistle, because she hastily explained. She had made some

calls and badgered the non-profit organization that ran the group home and a number of other downtown, mission-focused businesses for a truck and driver. A quick call next to the head priest at St. Paul's convinced him to lend her a trio of altar boys to help clean up.

— We can get most of the smoky smell from the clothes, too, for care baskets for needy families, she added.

Mrs. Nyman barked an order and her small army scurried into action. Everyone grabbed bags and boxes and relayed them to the truck at the curb. In minutes, the store had been emptied, leaving only the glaring lights, dusty shelves, skeletal racks, and soot-stained walls. One by one, we migrated outside with the last boxes and garbage bags, handing them to the tattooed guy in the back of the truck. The closing of the truck's cargo door echoed loudly against the now-empty storefronts along the Weston's facade.

My parents thanked everyone—even the embarrassed teenage boys—with handshakes and brief embraces. Before he and The Shirt left, Saul shuffled over and awkwardly returned my phone and the headphones. I put them in my pocket and thanked him for his help. He looked up from the sidewalk for an instant and smiled as his eyes found mine, and then he pressed something into my hands as he turned and made his awkward way back to his father's car. It was a cash receipt from the register, wrinkled and damp, with a short note on the back written in an unsteady, childlike hand:

I LIKE YOUR STORE.
I FEEL WELCOME HERE.
THANK YOU FOR LETTING ME VISIT.

After the vehicles pulled away, I handed Saul's note to my parents.

— That's nice, Dad said.

— More than nice, Mom said. It's— it's—

She didn't have to finish the thought.

I helped clean up the empty pizza boxes and fold the chairs. Dad and Mom said they were going upstairs to see about the smoke damage in the apartment. I walked back into Second Chances with the boxes, hoping to put them in the recycling bins out back. Mrs. Nyman stood next to the register, her shoulders stooped, her wrinkles deeper, as though the poised woman who had risen so mightily in support of Hamilton's poor had departed, replaced again by the sad, elderly lady who so often planted herself in front of the store. The silver box that the blond robber had returned sat on the counter. After his surrender I'd returned it to a shelf—we sold every Niche item, after all—but no one had bought it. I couldn't bring myself to box it up, either, and had laid it on the counter beside the cracked photograph of the building I'd retrieved from under the register.

She didn't notice that I had come back in. I laid the empty cardboard slabs on the far end of the counter and watched as she hooked her cane on the edge of the counter and picked up the box. She brought the gorgeous carvings to eye level and inspected them. Despite the fire, the little box was as brilliant as the day it had been returned, reflecting a hundred tiny sparks from the work lamps. She opened the clasp and looked into the empty silken interior as though expecting to find something there, before latching the box again and returning it to the counter.

— That little box, I said, is having quite a summer.

I'd lowered my voice, but she still started, her hand moving to her throat, where a small cry escaped.

— I'm so sorry, Mrs. Nyman—I didn't mean to frighten you.

— Don't worry about it. I was just lost in thought.

— It's a beautiful piece.

— It was my grandmother's.

— Really? How did it end up here?

— I put money inside and hid it in the baby's blanket, she said. I thought it could help him.

How do we measure the value of such things? My writer's curiosity begged me to interrogate her for even more detail, for the whole story. But I didn't, forcing myself to be content with connecting the pieces she'd offered weeks before to the continuing story of the precious little box, the only thing besides blood and genes she had been able to send with her infant son. And the Niche had brought it back to her. She began to cry in the musty air of our family store, her frail shoulders heaving. I lifted the silver box, cool and solid, and placed it her hand.

— Take it. It's yours.

She held it to her chest and left without another word. Some things can only be given and received as gifts.

I lifted the pizza boxes and walked to the back. My steps now echoed, uncomfortable and alien, blending with the gentle sounds of traffic along King sliding in through the open front door. Soft footsteps filtered down from the apartment above as my parents moved around, sounds that had always been inaudible before, absorbed by clothing and books and treasures. My father had finally managed to sand and paint the drywall compound over the bullet hole. He'd done such a good job that, apart from the memory, you'd never know it had been there at all.

After tossing the boxes on the recycling pile, I sat in Mom's old office chair, listening to the echoes from its stiff, creaky joints. The store wasn't completely empty—there were odd bits still strewn about, a pen here, a slip of lined paper there—but it felt that way. My mother was putting on a brave face about losing her inventory, but I wondered how she'd feel about seeing so much space when it had seemed so full, as if the store's merchandise had been an odd if ever-present kind of company.

Across the room, the Niche stood open on its hinges; I must have forgotten to close it after I took the kauri fiddlehead out. I could see right inside, its painted wood interior stark against the glare of the work lamps. I was tempted to close it, perhaps ready it to reveal its magic to whomever opened it next, but I didn't. I just stayed in the chair, parked next to Mom's steel surplus desk. The desk itself was free from the ever-present clutter that had always defined it, apart from three items: a vintage calculator, complete with faded chiclet keys, green-lit digits, and yellowing roll of register paper, a rag made from an old T-shirt crumpled and forlorn at the corner, and a green transit card precariously balanced at the desk's chipped edge. I picked up the card, turning it over in my hands a few times and wondering if it was the same card Peter had purchased for our outing to the fair. When I took out my phone, hoping to text him and tell him that we were finishing up, I saw that I'd already received one from him.

— *I luv U!!!!!!*

An attempt to cheer me up with abbreviated spelling and excessive exclamation points. Peter, my Peter, trying to be funny. Reaching me, forcing himself to stumble over the little things. I smiled.

Mom and Dad came down from the apartment a short while later and found me still sitting, lost in thought. They had been crying. I guess the sight of Wu's things scattered willy-nilly—everything had happened so quickly that the apartment looked like it usually had—shattered them. I knew it would do the same to me too, so I declined their offer to go upstairs and salvage anything I might need while we stayed on at the hotel. My journal could wait; I didn't see myself writing much for a while anyway. Mom looked around the store before suggesting we get out of there. I understood her well. She had been as quiet as the rest of us but managed to keep a brave face on for most of the day, even as we boxed up her livelihood. Standing in that empty space must have felt like being submerged in loss. She wiped her eyes and tried to brighten up, suggesting we have a family dinner over at Duster's before heading back to our suite.

— Can you text Leich? I can't even look at a phone right now.

— Sure, Mom.

— *hey, loser—*

I stopped tapping my screen, my old habits feeling not quite appropriate, like a shirt one size too small. I tried again.

— *were havng dinr at dusters. c u there?*

An instant response.

— *Yea! C u soon!*

I couldn't recall ever having seen him use an exclamation mark in his texts, much less two of them.

We hadn't been to Duster's as a family in quite some time, and never on a Friday. The place was packed, the after-work crowd swimming through happy hour. Jenny, surprised to see us, practically fell over herself to arrange a table, hurrying along a young couple. She yelled into the kitchen for Bart who, sweaty and stained with a cloth slung over his shoulder, came out to offer his sympathies.

Leich arrived as we were finishing our appetizers, looking fidgety. He motioned frantically at someone just out of view, and the calls and texts and strangely timed disappearances made sense when a cute, shy girl came over to endure a round of family introductions. She was polite, and it was obvious that my big brother was taken with her. He apologized for running out that morning, but he'd agreed to meet her family at lunch, and now it was her turn. There was an apology in his tone, too, for the timing of the introduction.

— We've wanted to tell you for a while, he said. But the last few days—

He was so eager. Her too. They watched Mom and Dad closely for their response. Mom's eyes filled—thinking of the son who'd never get the chance to date, no doubt—but she quickly wiped them, stood up, and hugged the startled girl.

— So you're the reason our boy has been so distracted, she said.

— It's really nice to meet you, the girl said.

Dad stood and pulled a chair over from an adjacent table.

— Please, sit, he said.

And she did. Leich practically melted with relief.

It was a wonderful meal. We stayed a long while, watching the after-work crowd dwindle, disappearing back to their cars and wherever they called home, before Friday-night customers, mostly downtown-dwellers lining up beside the taps, filled their spots. Jenny kept the door open the whole night, letting in the noises from the bar's small patio and the sounds of traffic along King. Mom and Dad asked me to extend an invitation to Peter, who walked right up to the table and pulled me into a huge embrace, complete with a quick kiss on the cheek for me and a grin for everyone else. We were surrounded by good people and that night was no exception. Leich's girlfriend and Peter laughed along with my family during light moments and held silence for the moments in which we remembered what we had lost. Jenny waved away the bill when my father offered to pay.

Although I held Peter's hand the whole time, I spent most of the night watching my family. Leich's hair had begun to grow over the scar and he had begun a scruffy attempt at a beard, undoubtedly for his new girlfriend. Through his grief he'd still found himself smitten, and I was happy for him. Mom and Dad, like the rest of us, were far from healed, but took advantage of the remarkable strength found in keeping company with those we love.

Wu was there, too, woven through the stories told in his name and brightening the smiles that dared remember his goodness. His mischievous eyes winked at us from the rims of every glass and bottle, his voice echoing in every swell of conversation and outburst of laughter. We got to hold him again. Or maybe we let him run down the sidewalk and play in the park, just out of sight, and climb all over the guns. Smiling. Pretending. Enjoying the cool of the iron against his wrinkled, perfect cheek.

TORONTO, NOW

The clock at the top of my screen tells me that I've again written myself into the deepest hours of the morning. I sit back from the computer, stretch, and rub my eyes. I'm not used to late nights anymore. Years ago, as a cub reporter always on call, I learned to survive by mastering open-eyed desk naps and throwing back double espressos in a single shot. My editor, who begrudgingly granted me a leave of absence a few weeks ago, often laughs at how soft I've become.

The kitchen table is now my home office, walled in by a dome of light from the overhead fixture. The rest of the apartment is dark, filled with the invisible white noise of nighttime, the hush of appliances and ductwork. Sleep sounds. Leich is on the couch, snoring. In the master bedroom down the hall, Peter will have shifted to my side of the bed, as though his resting self needs to keep it warm for me.

I won't sleep. You can tell a story and still not be ready for it. I'm in this strange limbo, caught between the satisfaction of knowing what has been accomplished and the unsettledness that comes from not knowing how this story will land, or on whom. Have I been fair to everyone involved?

— Is it even my story to tell?

At the sound of my voice, Leich grunts and rolls onto his side. I called him a few weeks ago and he dropped everything to help me, leaving his law practice and family behind in Vancouver. He fills in the inevitable gaps, the pieces I've forgotten. When I found myself unable to write he took over at the keyboard, giving me space when the words eluded me, when the details struggled to assemble themselves. It's not enough to say that I'm glad he's here— sometimes only a big brother can convince a little sister to carry more than she thinks she can.

A thick, white courier envelope sits on the table beside the computer. It arrived at my Toronto office months ago on the hottest day of the year. A sky so hazy you couldn't see it, just a wash of indistinct grey. Zero wind. The humidity like a wet shawl on the city's shoulders. Lake Ontario fading into the sky. My eighteenth-floor cubicle looks south, high enough on clear days to count plumes of steam rising from the Buffalo skyline. Clear or not, though, I can't see Hamilton—it's off to the west, blocked by skyscrapers and condos.

I pick the envelope up and hold it flat in my hands, feeling the weight of the two photographs and the letter inside. I must have slid them back into the envelope at some point, though I can't remember doing so. I think briefly of taking them out—not seeing my constant writing companions next to my computer feels odd.

I don't need the pictures or letter in my hand to know them. Corners curled upwards, edges dingy and worn from frequent handling, creased and smudged, branded by coffee-cup rings. One photo is the same grainy print of the Weston Arcade's King Street facade that hung behind our cash register. The other is more recent, a dusty candid of an excavator digging into the cornice overlooking Hughson Street. The walls look tired. Sooty eyeshadow spreads above every window, through which I can see light where light shouldn't be: the roof is gone. The letter is brief, written in The Shirt's tight, precise script.

> *Mutton, I'm afraid we've lost the Weston. After the fire, the building was inspected and determined to be too unstable to stand, taking most of the control out of our hands. To make matters worse, even as we petitioned City Hall for time and funding to save the facade, the demolition started this week, earlier than had been scheduled and begun without a permit. I should have fought harder. I'm so sorry.*

Amazing how three small pieces of paper can unlock twenty years of silence.

I turn back to the screen, willing myself to face a kind of ending. The events of that summer have never been far from my thoughts, of course, locked out of sight in a secret spot only I know. Safe but accessible. When I first saw that letter and those pictures, I was overcome by the need to tell our story. But the intensity of the past few weeks, the intimacy and pain of the details, have me wondering whether I should gather up my work and stash it away.

Leich won't let me. He'll say words like Legacy, Responsibility, the Importance of Preservation. He took the train to Hamilton a few days ago and was stunned by how prosperous the core has become, how bustle has supplanted need. The Shirt made good on his promise, forming a consortium of business owners with the mandate that protecting old buildings would bring good things to the city. After Wu's death, Dad decided to sell the Weston to the consortium and Mom, having decided not to reopen, let him. New businesses moved in, and for twenty years the Weston's old, handsome face hosted stores and shops and galleries, some flourishing, others not. Earlier this year, the fire mentioned in the letter—far hungrier than the one Peter braved on my behalf—spread quickly and gutted the building. We know how it began, roughly where the back room of our store once was, but not why; it was a painful gap in the history of the Weston, which along with a dozen other protected buildings had come to define the essence of a revitalized downtown.

Leich was also heartbroken. The Weston is in the final stages of demolition, barely visible behind safety walls and fencing. Duster's is long gone, replaced by an anonymous variation of the chain-sports-bar theme. The granite cenotaph, weathered by pollution and the friction of a thousand mourning hands, is now surrounded by an angular memorial space. Gore Park's trees have been cut down, creating more light and almost too much room. There are new, sterile concrete benches and paths that don't encourage people to linger. There'd be no spot for Satan's Falafel now.

The people have changed. More designer labels than thrift-store bargains, more hands holding lattes than double-doubles. The shelters and halfway houses trickled away as the rents increased, so those residents don't congregate around the park's fountain and on corners any more. People like Mrs. Nyman have had to find other places to rest and read their novels, other stretches of sidewalk where they might encourage fifteen-year-old city girls to dig deep and create.

I never finished the short story I agonized over that summer. Instead, a few days after my final Guild meeting after Wu's funeral—where Eleanor crafted a toast to me and my family that made even Bart cry—I found myself writing about Mrs. Nyman, the child she gave up, and the fine silver box she sent with him on his lonely journey. When the words came back, my river, swollen with everything that had happened to us, burst its banks. Mrs. Nyman's tiny snippets of truth became a story. After letting her read the draft—she loved it and simply asked that I change her name—I immediately wrote the next story. And the next. I never had to search for words again.

My writing carried me to university and a successful career in Toronto, and the faces of Hamilton faded. I lost touch with the Guild. The return address on The Shirt's letter is unfamiliar. I'd like to imagine him retiring to one of the downtown's stately century homes, still connected, but for all I know he and Saul found themselves in the suburbs. Mr. Ahmad retired his falafel cart when the city rezoned the park. I have no idea what became of Red and Blue, though I hope they were able to rise above their situation. The Outfit died under suspicious circumstances a few years ago; I like to imagine that no one misses him.

I turn towards the sound of bare feet on loose floor-boards. Peter blinks against the light and stands behind me.

— You're not sleeping, I say.

— I was. Well, dozing. Couldn't quite drop off.

He looks over at Leich

— He's not having any trouble.

— I'm almost finished. You should go back to bed—I don't know how long I'll be.

— I just wanted to see how you're doing.

Tell him, I think. Tell him about the need to finish but the uncertainty about what to do next. He'll encourage you to share it with others. Help you get past your hesitation. I stare at the blinking cursor on the screen but say nothing. After a moment, Peter yawns, scratches the stubble on his cheek, lays a quick hand on my shoulder.

— I'm glad you're getting to the end, he says.

— Me too.

He moves away, out of the light. I hear him pad down the hall and close our door behind him. I can still feel his hand on my shoulder.

How far we've come.

Part of me wants to go back. Walk around the old neighbourhood, visit the curbs, the sidewalks, the four corners nearest the Weston. I know our home is gone, but I miss the stairs leading up to our apartment, the kitchen window overlooking the park. The store. The mustiness of thrift-store things. The anticipation and ritual of the Niche's daily offering. Opening the door to the sidewalk, the smell of the mills, that low-slung haze from the smelters, hot and wrong and wonderful. But I won't go back. I can't imagine being in Hamilton without my complete family, just as I can't imagine completing this story without my big brother nearby.

Leich is comfortable in Vancouver. Mom, Dad, and I moved into another downtown apartment, smaller and with far too short a history, more existing than living. When I took my shot at Toronto—marrying Peter somewhere along the way—my parents had no reason to stay in Hamilton. They followed Leich out west, never too far away to drop in, which they often do. I visit when I can, but am more at peace in my own spaces and routines. I don't think that family closeness depends on proximity—if Leich ever needs me me, I'll drop everything, too—but grows best from a comfortable and necessary distance.

I return my fingers to the keyboard's rest positions. There are more words. There will always be more to say, to clarify, to add. Maybe I'll never stop working on it, make it my very own life project, like a vast needlepoint mosaic or an eternity quilt.

No.

In a few hours, when Leich and Peter wake up to face the day, I'll make sure they see the words The End in the expected location. They'll want to celebrate. Although I've been firm about not sharing this story with anyone other than our family, we'll again debate whether I should try to find a publisher. Leich will call Mom and Dad to tell them that we've laid the guns, the grief, and all those pre-chanced things to rest. I'll smile and say that yes, the story is done.

For now. Because if I've learned anything, it's that the most important stories never truly end. Especially the ones that take so long to tell in the first place.

ACKNOWLEDGMENTS

Thanks owed for the publication of this novel are legion, and I'm humbled by how much I've been given along the way. To God, for making every bit of it possible. To my parents, Bill and Grace van Staalduinen, who gave me structure and guidance and space, a miraculous balance. To Kirsten, Dennis, and Sharon, my stubborn and beautiful siblings, who make life better for everyone around them and shine so brightly along the way. To Leigh Nash and Invisible Publishing, who took a chance on a first novel and have been a true joy to work with. To my squad of intrepid first readers: Nicole Baute, Christina Farley, Heather Hughes, James Leck, Amanda Leduc, and Jane Vanden Berg. Special thanks go out to Hugh Cook, Wayne Grady, Annabel Lyon, and Michael Winter for previewing this work. To Chris Pannell, for lending me a few of his stunning words about our city. To the faculty and students in the creative writing program at UBC. To Roz Nay, for championing this novel's potential from the get-go. To the Ontario Arts Council and its legendary support of independent artists. To anyone not listed here but who has dug and prodded and inspired me to create, know that you're a part of this and my story. Thank you all.

Finally, while knowing there are no words that can adequately express my gratitude, I would like to thank my wife Rosalee, my living proof that I'm a part of a bigger narrative, for giving me limitless encouragement, as much time as I need to make my art, beautiful children, and more love than a guy can imagine. My Left, you make me better in every way. I love you.

INVISIBLE PUBLISHING is a not-for-profit publishing company that produces contemporary works of fiction, creative non-fiction, and poetry. We publish material that's engaging, literary, current, and uniquely Canadian. We're small in scale, but we take our work, and our mission, seriously: our titles are culturally relevant, well written, beautifully designed, and affordable.

We are committed to publishing diverse voices and experiences. In acknowledging historical and systemic barriers, and the limits of our existing catalogue, we strongly encourage Indigenous and writers of colour to submit their work.

Invisible Publishing has been in operation for almost a decade. Since releasing our first fiction titles in the spring of 2007, our catalogue has come to include works of graphic fiction and non-fiction, pop culture biographies, experimental poetry and prose.

Invisible Publishing continues to produce high-quality literary works, and we're also home to the Bibliophonic series, the Snare and Throwback imprints.

If you'd like to know more please get in touch:
info@invisiblepublishing.com

Invisible Publishing
Halifax & Toronto